QUEER BEATS

How the Beats Turned America On to Sex

edited by Regina Marler

CLEIS
PRESS

Published in the United States by Cleis Press Inc.,
P.O. Box 14684, San Francisco, California 94114.
Printed in the United States.
Cover design: Scott Idleman
Cover photograph: Students, writers, and friends Hal Chase, Jack Kerouac, Allen Ginsberg, and William S. Burroughs (L–R) enjoy each other's company in Morningside Heights, near the Columbia University campus in Manhattan. © Allen Ginsberg/CORBIS
Book design: Karen Quigg
Cleis Press logo art: Juana Alicia
First Edition.
10 9 8 7 6 5 4 3 2 1

LIBRARY OF CONGRESS CATALOGING-IN-PUBLICATION DATA

Queer beats : how the beats turned America on to sex / edited by Regina Marler.
                    p. cm.
ISBN 1-57344-188-0 (pbk.)
1. Homosexuality—Literary collections. 2. Authors, American—20th century—Biography. 3. Homosexuality and literature—United States. 4. Sexual orientation—Literary collections. 5. Beat generation—Literary collections. 6. Gay men—United States—Biography. 7. American literature—20th century. 8. Beat generation—Biography. 9. Sex—Literary collections. 10. Erotic literature, American. I. Marler, Regina, 1964–
        PS509.H57Q44 2004
        810.8'0353—dc22
                2004003828

For Davis

Acknowledgments

I would like to thank Don Weise for suggesting this book to me, and Ruth Davis, wherever you are, for giving me a paperback copy of *On the Road* as an entree to adulthood. To my publishers, Felice Newman and Frédérique Delacoste, thank you for your patience and good humor.

I am grateful to the following angels for offering information, guidance, support, and tender, loving care in the writing of *Queer Beats*: Peter Hale of the Ginsberg Trust; James Grauerholz of the William Burroughs estate; John Giorno; Harold Norse; Brenda Knight; Allen Young; M. DuBose; Ira Silverberg; Leo Skir; Holly Bemiss; Randy Wicker; Jack Nichols; Gina Allison; Renee Marler; and Paul Yamasaki of City Lights Bookstore. I'm sure this list is incomplete. If I've omitted any names here, it is unintentional.

This book would not be possible without the amazing critical and textual efforts of the scholars and writers who have preceded me in this rich field. I could not begin to name all the works I have drawn on in my study of the Beats, but I can say that my understanding of Burroughs was shaped by Oliver Harris's edition of his letters and by Jamie Russell's remarkable *Queer Burroughs*, that Ann Charter's *Portable Beat Reader* was my frequent companion, and that my sense of Ginsberg was guided by the twin lights of Barry Miles's definitive biography and Jane Kramer's skillful, devilish portrait, *Allen Ginsberg in America*. Anyone hoping to understand the Beats in the context of the 1950s would do well to begin with John D'Emilio's *Sexual Politics, Sexual Communities*, Diane di Prima's *Recollections of My Life as a Woman*, and Brenda Knight's *Women of the Beat Generation*.

Sooner murder an infant in its cradle than nurse unacted desires.

—WILLIAM BLAKE

Did I tell you about the rat who was conditioned to be queer by the shock and cold water treatment every time he makes a move at a female? He says: "Mine is the love that dare not squeak its name."

—WILLIAM BURROUGHS

CONTENTS

III. Queer Shoulder to the Wheel

Introduction

In the summer of 1948, Allen Ginsberg sublet a Spanish Harlem apartment from a fellow student at Columbia University and began reading the theology books stacked around the room in orange crates. In a mystical frame of mind, he pored over William Blake, Saint Teresa of Avila, Saint John of the Cross. One afternoon, he lay on the bed by the open window, his pants unzipped, reading Blake's "Ah! Sunflower" while masturbating. After he came, he heard a low, ancient voice that seemed to emanate from somewhere in the room. It was the voice of Blake himself, he realized, reciting his own poem. "The peculiar quality of the voice was something unforgettable," Ginsberg later explained, "because it was like God had a human voice, with all the infinite tenderness and mortal gravity of a living Creator speaking to his son." The vision persisted, accompanied by heightened visual perception and a sudden knowledge of the wondrous complexity of nature and the divine significance of the works of man: "I had the impression of the entire universe as poetry filled with light and intelligence and communication and signals."

The dead poet read other verses from *Songs of Innocence* and *Songs of Experience*, in each of which Ginsberg now saw himself as the subject. He was the rose in "The Sick Rose" and Lyca, the girl, in "The Little Girl Lost." As the vision faded, he stumbled, ecstatic, onto the fire escape and shouted into the neighboring apartment, "I've seen God!" The two girls inside slammed the window shut. Later, his psychoanalyst hung up on him. He told his father, too, who worried that Ginsberg was showing signs of the schizophrenia that had caused his mother to be hospitalized.

For the next fifteen years, Ginsberg would try to re-create this rapturous experience through the use of drugs of every kind, even journeying alone to the jungles of Peru in search of a hallucinogen called *yage,* used by witch doctors. The Blake vision was so pivotal for Ginsberg that several versions of the story exist,* in all of which his pants are open but in none of which does Ginsberg or his interviewer think to remark on this. The masturbation is an integral part of the scene; including it is as natural, for Ginsberg, as describing the brilliant blue of the sky outside the apartment window. So effectively did he project in his writings his sense of these transporting moments and their lasting significance—and so powerfully did his sensibility alter the world around him—that by the time he gave the 1966 *Paris Review* interview from which I've drawn these quotes, his open fly was a mundane detail. He'd helped create a culture in which references to a hand on a cock can go without notice.

This candid attitude toward sex and the body—toward pleasure in general—is one of the enduring legacies of the Beat writers, though only Ginsberg would fulfill this ideal to the extent of appearing naked at parties full of clothed people. Theirs was a revolution of flesh as well as the word. The orgies, addictions, and all-night Benzedrine-fueled writing binges of Beat legend are, in the end, inseparable from their search for the ultimate reality of the kind embodied in the Blake vision or in the high-speed, cross-country road trips immortalized in Jack Kerouac's *On the Road.*

Those who read beyond the legend know that Kerouac retreated to a paranoid conservatism in his forties, that the openly gay Ginsberg, even in midlife, often longed for a wife and children, and that William Burroughs would sometimes, when kicking a drug addiction, claim that he wanted cunt, that he was never meant to be queer. These are the

* In retelling the story here, I rely on Barry Miles's *Ginsberg: A Biography* (New York: Simon & Shuster, 1989).

contradictions of actual lives, of midcentury lives in particular. The Beat writers did not always bring these conflicts into their works, though they aired them in conversation and letters. This open confession of their feelings was one of the pivots of the movement, and no less vital to their influence on the rising counterculture than their marijuana reveries and restless experiments in literary form.

The group's origins lay in friendships formed at and around Columbia, in upper Manhattan, in the months after Christmas 1943, when Allen Ginsberg, then a freshman, met a raffish, angelic-looking aesthete named Lucien Carr. It was the sophisticated Carr who first took Ginsberg down to Greenwich Village to meet "queer and interesting people," as Ginsberg wrote to his brother Eugene, adding that he planned to try to get drunk. Soon after this walk on the wild side, Carr introduced him to Jack Kerouac, an ex-Columbia football player and aspiring writer, and Dave Kammerer, an older gay man whose life was organized around a hopeless love for Carr that dated from Carr's childhood in Saint Louis. At Kammerer's place, they met another exile from Saint Louis: William Burroughs, a thirty-year-old Harvard graduate and escapee from respectability whose friends included petty thieves, hipsters, junkies, and Times Square hustlers, like Herbert Huncke,* as well as a number of pretty boys, immortalized in Kerouac's *Visions of Cody* as "the Sensualists." Along with higher-minded works like the philosophy of Spengler, the novels of Genet were among the first books Burroughs passed on to his younger friends. He led them around Times Square— Kerouac in terror—in and out of gay bars. Burroughs made no secret of his orientation—he had cut off the tip of a finger to impress one piece of trade—but Ginsberg was still unsure of his. A virgin with both men and women, he had fallen in love with the golden-haired and irredeemably straight Lucien Carr, and then with Kerouac, too. The friends indulged

---

* The underworld charm of Huncke can probably be summed up by the opening of his sketch "Elsie John": "Elsie John, the hermaphrodite, was my introduction to narcotics. He was working West Madison Street in a freak show—half man, half woman."

in marathon, late-night arguments in cafeterias, drank hard, discovered drugs. Kerouac, who had lost his best friend in the war that spring, was hungry for intensity, for purity. In his own blood, he copied out a Nietzsche quotation: "Art is the highest task and the proper metaphysical activity of this life."*

Given the group's respect for any expression of individuality or risk-taking, it comes as no surprise that one of the galvanizing moments in the emergence of the Beat identity was a gay murder. On the night of August 13, 1944, Lucien Carr stabbed Dave Kammerer in a drunken argument and tried to sink his body in the Hudson River. Theirs had been a strange romance. Like a spoiled child, Carr bullied and tormented Kammerer, yet never put him off decisively. They were drinking buddies, with something of the young Rimbaud and his adoring Verlaine in their stormy relationship, though they were apparently never lovers. That night, after leaving a bar, Carr and Kammerer had walked to the river with a bottle. Kammerer professed his love again and threatened to kill them both. Driven to rage, Carr stabbed him over and over with a Boy Scout knife. "I just killed the old man," said Carr, knocking on Burroughs's door at dawn and handing him a blood-stained pack of Lucky's.

"The act seemed to have a gratuitous grace," as John Tytell wrote in *Naked Angels*. "It was an exemption from the ordinary, a romantic gauntlet in the bland face of the world." With his grim insight into human nature, Burroughs felt that Kammerer had been asking for it, demanding a consummation of one kind or another. Although considered an "honor killing" by newspapers and police—Carr was straight, after all, and Kammerer queer—Carr went to prison for two years on a first-degree manslaughter charge, and Kerouac was arrested, though later released, for helping his friend dispose of the murder weapon. Ginsberg wrote in his journal, "The libertine circle is destroyed with the death of Kammerer." In fact, the group was brought closer. It had lost Carr, however, who emerged from prison a solid citizen, who would go

* Ann Charters, ed., *Jack Kerouac: Selected Letters, 1940–1956* (New York: Viking, 1995), 81.

through life annoyed by his friends' "dig-up-of-the-past, roll-in-your-own-shit" writings.* He remained friendly with Ginsberg and the others, but the spark of their early association had gone out.

Carr was replaced, to some extent, by Joan Vollmer Adams, a brainy, charismatic journalism student whose large apartment on West 115th Street became home to many of the Beats for the next two years. Separated from her husband, but with a new baby girl, she was an unlikely housemother—and an unlikely mother, too, who ran through young men, had a haphazard way with birth control, and, when introduced to Benzedrine by Kerouac, quickly became addicted. Ginsberg's classmate Hal Chase was an early tenant of hers. Ginsberg moved in after getting kicked out of Columbia in spring 1945, and Kerouac shared a room there with Edie Parker, whom he had hastily married after the Kammerer murder. The last to move in was William Burroughs, for whom Joan had saved the best room. Their intellectual connection was as strong as any Burroughs had experienced with male friends; it was Joan, for example, who suggested that Mayan priests must have practiced mind control—a theory that recurs, in altered forms, throughout his later writings. They developed an almost telepathic union. Burroughs's preference for men seemed irrelevant when they fell into bed. Joan told him he made love like a pimp.

In the wake of the Kammerer stabbing, Ginsberg had confessed his attraction to Kerouac, whose first response was a genial rejection. His second response was to exchange furtive hand jobs with Ginsberg one night under the elevated railway. The murder had shocked Ginsberg out of the closet, as Kerouac biographer Dennis McNally puts it. Although he had had a few unsatisfying encounters with strangers over the next year, he yearned for a lover.

* As well as later mentions in *Howl* and elsewhere, Kerouac and Burroughs quickly banged out a 200-page pulp account of the murder, called *And the Hippos Were Boiled in Their Tanks*. Carr made them swear never to publish it. Kerouac's account of the murder, *Vanity of Duluoz*, wasn't published until 1968. Even Ginsberg tried to write a novel about the incident for a creative writing course at Columbia but was dissuaded by the assistant dean.

Neal Cassady was a Denver friend of Hal Chase's—a twenty-year-old street kid and ex-con who could hot-wire a Ford or a schoolgirl in a matter of seconds. He had grown up in and out of skid row hotels with his wino father, with a long stint in reform school. Handsome, athletic, self-taught, a brilliant, rapid-fire talker who peppered his conversation with quotes from Proust and the "yes yes yes" of perpetual motion, he took the group of friends by storm when he visited them with his sixteen-year-old girlfriend, LuAnne, in the fall of 1946. In this manic, sexually voracious "maverick of inspiration," Ginsberg found what he'd been looking for. And so, unexpectedly, did Jack Kerouac. Hearing rumors about this wild man, Kerouac went to meet him. Cassady opened the door naked, with a hard on, having leapt out of bed with LuAnne.

And so arrived the muse. In *On the Road*, Kerouac described Ginsberg's first meeting with Cassady: "Two piercing eyes glanced into two piercing eyes—the holy con-man with the shining mind, and the sorrowful poetic con-man with the dark mind."* One night in January 1947, Ginsberg and Cassady shared a bed, and Cassady graciously initiated sex. Their attraction was genuine and mutual, though not lasting for Cassady. "Neal was a hard guy to get to know intimately," Herbert Huncke later wrote, "because he lived very much within himself, as gung-ho as he was."** Because he was predominantly heterosexual—and faithful to no one—Cassady became a painful obsession for Ginsberg. For years after, on visits to Cassady, he would try to re-create the closeness of those first weeks. Ginsberg soon began to explore his conflicted feelings about his emerging sexual identity in poems like "In Society" (1947), in which he peeks inside a meat sandwich at a gay party and finds that it contains a dirty asshole. The pain of Cassady's rejection reinforced all his fears about living a queer life. Only two months after the affair with Cassady began (with Cassady, writing from Denver again, wildly backtracking on his physical attraction to men), Ginsberg wrote

* *On the Road* (New York: Signet, 1982), 8.
** *Guilty of Everything* (New York: Paragon House, 1990), 94.

to Wilhelm Reich, at Burroughs's suggestion, asking him to recommend an analyst for his "psychic difficulty" as a homosexual.

To Kerouac, Cassady was both a brother and a muse. Any careful reading of Kerouac's novels or his published letters reveals a sensitive and gentle mama's boy who goaded himself into macho displays. The most conventional of the group—and the one whose queer sensibility was most disguised, folded into the hero worship of *On the Road* and *Visions of Cody*—it's no accident he's also the most popular of the Beat writers. His alter ego in *On the Road* is the narrator, Sal Paradise, but readers have often associated him with the womanizing Cassady character, Dean Moriarty.

Despite his three marriages and the impressive amount of girlie action recorded in his notebooks, Kerouac had a long history of casual queer sex.* He and Gore Vidal "rubbed bellies," among other parts, in one of the most famous pairings New York's Chelsea Hotel has seen. Harold Norse remembers finding Kerouac on the bed in Chester Kallman's apartment after another brief encounter. His close friend Ginsberg may have been his only long-term male sex partner, with Ginsberg providing the occasional blow job and ego boost. Kerouac was clearly sexually attracted to Neal Cassady, the central figure of two of his novels, but it was Cassady's frontier masculinity that he admired—his casual dominance of women, his self-assurance, his prowess. A sexuality that would have appeared frenzied to a laid-back cat like Burroughs was a thing of beauty to Kerouac, who declared that, for Cassady, sex was "the one and only holy and important thing in life."** His line in *Visions of Cody* about Cassady masturbating six times a day slips into every Beat biography. Although Kerouac knew about his new friend's gay hustling and his affair with Ginsberg, Cassady was his "phallic totem," as John Tytell styled it, and there is little chance that Kerouac would have

* Gerard Nicosia's biography *Memory Babe* documented his bisexuality, and Ellis Amburn's *Subterranean Kerouac* (1998) exhaustively outed him, attributing his writer's block, his bigotry, and the drunken belligerence of his later years to his refusal to accept his homosexuality.
** *On the Road*, 6.

threatened either his own self-image or his idealization of Cassady by acting on his attraction.

Kerouac's only sex with Cassady was by proxy, through the time-honored act of sharing women. Cassady's discarded or neglected girlfriends proved easy pickups for the handsome Kerouac. And in spring 1952, Cassady encouraged an affair between Kerouac and his second wife, Carolyn, in part to add the spice of jealousy to his marriage and in part to connect on a deeper level with his friend. In her memoir, *Heartbeat*, Carolyn describes Jack as a tender and attentive lover, a welcome contrast to her brutish husband. But Kerouac was never able to form a lasting bond with any of the women he loved. As the writer Steven Watson summed up his relationships with women: "He became infatuated with a woman associated with a male buddy; he fantasized domesticity; he drove away in a car; he proposed marriage; he returned to his mother."* Kerouac rushed through the stages of romantic love as if reading a book in one night: from attraction through jealous possession to disenchantment and a sense of being trapped (a rapid progression perfectly described in *The Subterraneans*). Then, when he had lost the prize, he succumbed to a brief, wrenching despair and, if he was lucky, banged out a new novel. In the ugliest chapter of his life, he denied paternity of his infant daughter, Jan, in 1952 and left her and her mother without support.**

Of the three principal Beat writers, only Kerouac identified as straight. "I never was, nor wanted to be, homosexual," he wrote in protest to an early piece of Beat criticism. Although his novels were all different in style and tone, his public image was based on his aggressively straight second novel, *On the Road*. For publication, Kerouac had been

* Steven Watson, *The Birth of the Beat Generation* (New York: Pantheon, 1995), 140.
** Railing against the government agency that was intent on hunting him down for child abandonment, he told Ginsberg: "there're one million men in this country trying never to see their wives again and these socialistic think-they're-well-meaning-pricks are trying to 'solve' that." (Charters, ed., *Selected Letters*, 344.) In his defense, Kerouac did believe that an earlier bout of mumps had left him sterile, and that the baby could not be his.

obliged to cut some gay content, but left in a few derisive references to fags and fairies, as well as one memory in which Sal Paradise, having failed to make it with a girl in San Francisco, notes that "there were plenty of queers":

> Several times I went to San Fran with my gun and when a queer approached me in a bar john I took out the gun and said, "Eh? Eh? What's that you say?" He bolted. I've never understood why I did that; I knew queers all over the country. It was just the loneliness of San Francisco and the fact that I had a gun. I had to show it to someone.*

Despite the urge to show off his gun, Kerouac was well aware of the dangers of revealing his bisexual inclinations. In a letter to Neal Cassady, he railed against queerness, then explained that he did so because he didn't want "posterity" to think he was queer. He wanted the behavior, clearly, but not the identity. And because he was able to distance himself from those opportunistic sex acts with men, he was in some ways less homophobic than Burroughs and Ginsberg in those early years. He wasn't forced to reconcile his self-image with the stereotype of the contemptible, effeminate American gay man.

In 1949, Ginsberg was hospitalized for seven months in the Columbia Presbyterian Psychiatric Institute on 168th Street. His internment had been part of a deal to keep him out of jail after an almost-comic escapade with Herbert Huncke and his friends, who had fled from the police in a car full of stolen goods. Ginsberg was also in the car, along with a box full of his most intimate letters, which he'd thought it unwise to keep in his apartment, where Huncke was storing booty as conspicuous as a cigarette machine. It seemed obvious to his doctors that Ginsberg was sick: his mother was mad; he was confessing to visions; his friends were

* *On the Road*, 62.

thieves and queers. Any reasonable cure, by the standards of the day, would include sexual reorientation.* With that in mind, Ginsberg emerged from prison a "straight" man and embarked on a five-year program of sexual conformity. He wrote to Kerouac of his relief at losing his virginity to a woman:

> I wandered around in the most benign and courteous stupor of delight at the perfection of nature; I felt the ease and relief of knowledge that all the maddening walls of heaven were finally down, that all my aching corridors were traveled out of, that all my queerness was camp, unnecessary, morbid, so lacking in completion and sharing of love as to be almost as bad as impotence and celibacy, which it almost was anyway.**

This is less a paean to hetero bliss than a poignant statement of the pain of being queer in the postwar period. Adhering to the advanced thought of the day, Ginsberg continually consulted psychologists and analysts in his search for a cure, until a San Francisco doctor finally told him he should do exactly as he pleased.

The Beat-associated poet Harold Norse's autobiography, *Memoirs of a Bastard Angel*, describes the agony of wanting to be normal, to be accepted. He remembers talking in the 1940s with his friend Tennessee Williams about "the problem of being queer": " 'It's a curse,' I said, 'the worst fate that could befall anyone. We have to hide our need for love and sex, never knowing when we might be insulted, abused, attacked, killed.' " Williams answered him in a choked voice. " 'Homosexuals,' " he said, " 'are wounded, deeply hurt. We live with a psychic wound that never heals.' " ***

---

* Even Burroughs, who had tried to psychoanalyze both Ginsberg and Kerouac while they lived at Joan Burroughs's apartment, and had reassured Ginsberg about his feelings for men, later told Ginsberg that a completely successful analysis would of course cure homosexuality.

** Quoted in Miles, 129.

*** *Memoirs of a Bastard Angel* (New York: Morrow, 1989), 128.

William Burroughs's response to the psychic wound was to flip the bird at bourgeois values. Attracted from childhood to vice of all kinds, he had been planning a robbery (never executed) at the time he met Ginsberg and Kerouac. When a box of stolen morphine syrettes and a shotgun came into his possession, he asked for help from some junky acquaintances in learning how to shoot up. Although he sold most of the syrettes, his addiction began at that point, both in his intellectual curiosity and in his attraction to the underworld. At a time in which homosexuality was regarded as criminal or pathological, Burroughs was smoothly formulating his conviction that there was no such thing as criminal behavior, only acts declared illegal by a particular society. In fact, if the modest, buttoned-down advocates of "homophile rights"— closeted schoolteachers, librarians, theater workers—had made more headway in this period, Burroughs in particular might have been far less attracted to the same-sex world. "I glanced through a book called *The Homosexual in America*," he wrote Ginsberg from Mexico in 1952, "Enough to turn a man's gut."

> This citizen says a queer learns humility, learns to turn the other cheek, and returns love for hate. Let him learn that sort of thing if he wants to. I never swallowed the other cheek routine, and I hate the stupid bastards who won't mind their own business. They can die in agony for all I care.*

The problem was that Burroughs, a self-professed "manly type" and gun freak, could not find a model for male homosexuality that didn't sicken him. His second novel, *Queer*, is a record of his loneliness and isolation, a man's man among expatriate fairies in Mexico City. He repudiated that book when he began to write *Naked Lunch,* the series of surreal, violent, and brilliantly inventive sketches ("routines")—some based on

* The book was by Donald Webster Cory. Oliver Harris, ed., *The Letters of William Burroughs, 1945–1958* (New York: Viking, 1993), 106.

letters to Ginsberg—that would make his name. Although he longed for a profound connection, a union of souls, he was forced to settle, much of his life, for brief, uneven affairs with younger men—often with trade—and a close circle of male friends. "He was divided between a puritan obsession with dirty sex and his own true romantic nature," writes his biographer Ted Morgan. In the wake of a failed romance in Mexico, Burroughs developed a passion for Allen Ginsberg that went largely unrequited. Not until the late 1950s did Burroughs connect with Ian Sommerville, who would be his lover and friend for the next seventeen years.

The 1940s and 1950s in America were hardly a steady march toward enlightenment, but they were not as uniformly repressive as pop history suggests. Many of the best-selling and most talked-about writers of the period were publishing gay-themed work: among them Truman Capote (*Other Voices, Other Rooms*, 1948), Gore Vidal (*The City and the Pillar*, 1948), Tennessee Williams (early plays and the story collection *One Arm*, 1948), and James Baldwin (*Giovanni's Room*, 1956). That mainstream publishers were willing to risk their reputations on gay-themed writing reflects the social changes brought about by the war—the beginnings of racial desegregation, geographic and social mobility, the educational benefits of the G.I. Bill, the expanded horizons of service men and women who'd been plucked from soda fountain stools in Grand Rapids or Tucson to serve tours of duty in places like postwar Paris or Tokyo.*

Despite the revelations of the Kinsey Report, the first volume of which, *Sexual Behavior in the Human Male*, was published in January 1948, conventional depictions of gay life remained censorious and stereotypical.** Even a close friend of Kerouac's, John Clellon Holmes,

* "With the stress of dislocation and impending doom," Norse recalled, "almost anyone in uniform was available.[...] Far from their home communities, unhindered by what others thought, most responded willingly to homosexual acts." *Memoirs of a Bastard Angel*, 105.
** Kinsey's statistics revealed that thirty-seven percent of American men surveyed had participated in homosexual acts ("leading to orgasm") in adulthood. His much-maligned study had the contradictory effects of normalizing queer sex while sparking political and religious outrage, military witch-hunts, and police crackdowns against gays.

who wrote the first article on the Beat Generation,* was incapable of seeing beneath the surface of what seemed a pathetic imitation of heterosexuality. His novel *Go* (1952) is the first fictional treatment of the Beats. In it, he described a visit to a Greenwich Village lesbian bar with all the lurid glow of a pulp novel:

> The Lesbians were in couples, the "men," brutal, comradely, coarse; wearing badly cut business suits and loud ties. The "girls" were carbon copies, except for long hair and dresses. The bar was filled with raucous jokes, back slapping and the suck of cigarettes. A few graceful, shoulder swinging homosexuals glided in from the street, mincing, chirruping and trying to rub up against everyone. "Christ, let's get out of here!" Ketchum explained with unusual heat. "It's horrible."**

The butches are not even allowed good tailoring.

Many gay writers addressed the subject only obliquely. Some, like Truman Capote, cultivated a camp voice and sensibility to tell stories that were not necessarily gay; some hid behind ambiguous pronouns (like early Frank O'Hara) or classical allusions. Many wrote openly, but then edited the most overt gay content out of the published versions of their work, as James Baldwin did in *Go Tell It on the Mountain* (1953). And of course many relied on unthreatening stereotypes of pale, willowy men tormented with obsessive love, yet still able to identify a Meissen tea service at fifty paces. Gore Vidal's *The City and the Pillar* was groundbreaking in its matter-of-fact tone and manly central characters, but he did not ruin his political aspirations by actually coming out.

The implicit argument behind sympathetic mainstream gay novels and poetry is that same-sex love is like any other, and that homosexuals

---

* The term "beat" was a piece of street jargon the friends picked up from Herbert Huncke, with the now-familiar meaning of "worn out, rejected." In one of his associative riffs, Kerouac expanded its definition to include "upbeat, beatific." Hope and degradation were thus entwined.
** *Go* (New York: Simon & Schuster, 1952), 95.

deserve the same respect and opportunities as anyone else. The works of the Beat writers stand outside this tradition. Theirs is the rebellious, confessional, ecstatic message of the shadow tradition: writers like Blake, Shelley, Whitman, Rimbaud, Céline, Henry Miller, Genet. Poet-prophets, seers and visionaries, outlaws, pornographers. "I want to get a wild page," Ginsberg wrote to the poet John Hollander in a fierce, long-winded defense of his poetry, "as wild and as clear (really clear) as the mind—no forcing the thoughts into straight jacket—sort of a search for the rhythm of the thoughts & their natural occurences & spacings & notational paradigms."*

However clearly they saw the political issues of their day, neither Ginsberg nor Burroughs were social realists in their work. When they wrote about being queer, they didn't focus on finding or making a place for queers within society. This is perhaps the chief distinction between them and the few other openly gay writers of the 1940s through the early 1960s: they were not assimilationist. If the culture would not accept them, the fault lay in the culture. By way of contrast, the Los Angeles branch of the Mattachine Society issued a statement in 1953 that "Homosexuals are not seeking to overthrow or destroy any of society's existing institutions, laws or mores, but to be assimilated as constructive, valuable, and responsible citizens"—a hopelessly square view that couldn't contrast more dramatically with Ginsberg's progressive politics, or Burroughs's disdain for social norms.** It isn't the gay content alone that made the work of Ginsberg and Burroughs and Kerouac controversial, but rather its unapologetic outsider status: its rejection of literary conventions and cold-war hysteria, its celebration of low life, its spiritual searching, its sexual explicitness.***

* Quoted in Tytell, 218.
** John D'Emilio, *Sexual Politics, Sexual Communities: The Making of a Homosexual Minority in the United States, 1940–50* (Chicago: Univ. of Chicago Press, 1983), 84.
*** For the most part, these were qualities shared with straight (or usually straight) Beat and Beat-associated writers like Michael McClure, Gary Snyder, Gregory Corso, Lawrence Ferlinghetti, and Diane di Prima.

And, obviously, its obscenity. The San Francisco censorship trial for Ginsberg's first book, *Howl*, made the author, the Beats, the poem, and the little bookstore that published it famous. Lawrence Ferlinghetti, owner of City Lights Bookstore in North Beach, had passed on a previous collection of verse that Ginsberg—the new poet in town—had given him. A now legendary poetry reading at Six Gallery on October 13, 1955, changed that. Ginsberg's inspired, incantatory recitation of the first part of *Howl*, accompanied by clapping and outbursts from the audience and Kerouac's drunken shouts of "Go!" and "Yeah!" and "So there!," was so convincing a demonstration of a powerful new voice that Ferlinghetti sent a telegram the next morning, asking for the manuscript. Years later, Ginsberg remembered Kerouac's telling him, "This poem, *Howl*, will make you famous in San Francisco," and Kenneth Rexroth correcting him: " 'No, this poem will make you famous from bridge to bridge,' which sounded like hyperbole, but I guess it did."*

City Lights's fourth publication in the Pocket Poets series, *Howl* was moderately well-received when it appeared in October 1956. Ginsberg went to great lengths to promote the book—as he did with his friends' work as well—but nothing had a greater effect than the sight of two plainclothes policemen buying copies at City Lights and promptly arresting the salesclerk, Shigeyoshi Murao. Ferlinghetti, too, was issued an arrest warrant. The trial was set for August 1957.

Ginsberg was not even in the country. He and his lover, Peter Orlovsky, followed the trial from Paris, in magazines like *Life*, where they caught sight of Neal Cassady in a courtroom photo. In October, Judge Clayton Horn declared that despite "coarse and vulgar language" and the mention of sex acts, the poem was not lacking in redeeming social importance—the crucial legal measure of obscenity as established in the *Ulysses* verdict. By the end of the trial, more than 10,000 copies of *Howl* were in print. Ginsberg found himself deluged with fan mail, and

* Jane Kramer, *Allen Ginsberg in America* (New York: Fromm, 1997), 48. (First published in 1969.)

when he returned to the States in July 1958, it was to sell-out audiences for his readings.

The censorship trials for *Naked Lunch* brought international attention to the Beats. Although the book was initially turned down by Maurice Girodias, founder of Olympia Press in Paris, and by Ferlinghetti, who found it "disgusting," excerpts appeared in 1959 in *Black Mountain Review* and the *Chicago Review*—the latter folded, in fact, after protests over Burroughs's work. "Also I was denounced in *The Nation* as an international homo and all around sex fiend," Burroughs wrote to Ginsberg. Relentless in his admiration for Burroughs, Irving Rosenthal, the gay former editor of the *Chicago Review*, published further excerpts in a new magazine, *Big Table*, which was held up by the Chicago postmaster general. At the *Big Table* trial, Judge Julius Hoffman—later to preside over the Chicago Seven trial—ruled that Burroughs's obscenities violated "a cultural and social taboo, to be sure, but not the law."* The notoriety that these legal squabbles gained for *Naked Lunch* encouraged Girodias to reconsider his decision not to publish. He gave Burroughs ten days to cobble together a finished draft from the many unordered scenes he had been carrying around for years.

Soon Barney Rosset of Grove Press, who had staked his fortune on publishing unexpurgated editions of banned books, like *Lady Chatterley's Lover*, approached Girodias. Despite the Paris publisher's eagerness to start a stream of royalties, the American edition of *Naked Lunch* would not appear until 1962, after Rosset won a tremendous legal battle to publish Henry Miller's *Tropic of Cancer*. As expected, a Boston bookseller was arrested for selling *Naked Lunch*. Ginsberg was instrumental in helping craft a defense strategy for the trial that followed in January 1965. Six expert witnesses were called, including Norman Mailer. As the shaggy-bearded final witness, Ginsberg, took the stand, the judge told him to straighten his collar. Undaunted, Ginsberg spoke for an hour,

* Quoted in Ted Morgan, *Literary Outlaw: The Life and Time of William S. Burroughs* (New York: Holt, 1988), 298.

passionately explaining the book's structure and significance. In the end, without a single witness for the prosecution, the judge declared *Naked Lunch* obscene. He said that Burroughs, "under the guise of portraying the hallucinations of a drug addict, had ingeniously satisfied his personal whims and fantasies, and inserted in this book hard-core pornography." *

This decision was successfully appealed before the Massachusetts Supreme Court in 1966, to the shock and delight of the defense witnesses. As Edward de Grazia, the attorney for Barney Rosset and Grove Press, wrote: "the *Howl, Tropic of Cancer,* and *Naked Lunch* decisions changed the literary landscape of America for good." ** The trials helped establish Ginsberg as a public figure. And the Beats were now associated not only with bohemianism but also with the rising culture of protest.

Although the number of full-time hipsters and Beatniks—the term coined by *San Francisco Chronicle* columnist Herb Caen in 1958 to describe the style revolution sweeping American campuses and cities—was still small, a Beat candidate ran for President in 1960, a psychiatric conference was held on the Beats at which Ginsberg spoke, and countless articles and television news stories discussed the new bohemians. "Even where homosexuality was not specifically mentioned," wrote the gay historian John D'Emilio, "writers almost invariably referred to sexual experimentation, promiscuity, orgies, and hedonism when describing the beats." *** After the Paris publication of *Naked Lunch*, when a *Life* article blasted the Beat writers as talentless, drug-addicted degenerates, Burroughs's aging mother wrote to him promising to keep up his stipend as long as he stayed away. He responded dryly: "Personally I would prefer to avoid publicity, but it is the only way to sell books." † In 1960, FBI director J. Edgar Hoover declared the Beatniks the third greatest threat to America, right after Communists and eggheads.

* Edward de Grazia "Allen Ginsburg, Norman Mailer, Barney Rosset: Their Struggles Against Censorship Recalled," *Cardozo Life* (New York: Yeshiva University, Fall 1998).
** Ibid.
*** D'Emilio, 181.
† Quoted in Morgan, 320.

Most of the press coverage of the Beats was in appalled reaction to their works, their lives, their personal grooming. It highlighted the gap between Beat values and those of the population at large, but had, of course, the effect of destabilizing the culture, since the Beats looked surprisingly content with their marginal position. Publicity also brought new readers to the Beat and Beat-related writers, many of whom—Denise Levertov, Harold Norse, Gary Snyder, LeRoi Jones, Michael McClure, to name a few—were poet-activists, committed, like Ginsberg, to poetry as an instrument of social change.* Later, Ginsberg came to regard *Howl* as "a crucial moment of breakthrough, [...] a breakthrough in the sense of a public statement of feelings and emotions and attitudes."** The first step in the revolution was to speak openly.

The Beat writers' influence on the nascent gay rights movement is seen most notably in this open avowal of orientation, of acts, of fantasies—the Beat sensibility of friendship (and the influence of Ginsberg's many attempts at "the talking cure") extending itself to their writings. Viewing the Beat oeuvre as a whole, Burroughs's *Queer* (written in 1952) is the transitional work, as much about queer anxiety as about desire, and full of a cringing awareness of the social taint of homosexuality. Even so, it proved too hot for Ace Books, publisher of the author's first novel, *Junkie*, and was then suppressed by him until 1985.*** So *Howl*—though written later—is the watershed: defiantly joyous and affirming, a Blakean thunderbolt of pride and indignation hurled at the repressions of the Eisenhower era. Nowhere else in the mid-1950s could gay male readers find such powerful, unabashed depictions of gay sex. As John D'Emilio argues: "Through the beats' example, gays could perceive

---

* Here is where they parted ways with Jack Kerouac, who had described, in a 1948 interview, the Beat "weariness with all the forms, all the conventions of the world." But near the end of his life, in a famous drunken appearance on *Firing Line* with William F. Buckley, he sounded more like his father: "As a Catholic, I believe in order, tenderness, and piety."
** Allen Young's *Gay Sunshine* interview, published 1973.
*** *Visions of Cody*, the more adoring of Kerouac's fictional reveries on Neal Cassady, was published posthumously in 1972, by which time its homoerotic content and reveries on masturbation were less challenging to readers.

themselves as nonconformists rather than deviates, as rebels against stultifying norms rather than immature, unstable personalities."* Ironically, Ginsberg had felt so free when writing *Howl* because he assumed it would never be published. He didn't want to embarrass his father with evidence of his immature, unstable personality.

Ginsberg had helped his mother sell chickpeas to benefit Israel during Communist Party meetings in the 1930s. He had entered Columbia hoping to become a labor lawyer. It was inevitable, perhaps, that his verse should become political—especially after he found both his subject matter and his form in *Howl*—and perhaps also inevitable that in the end, his public life would undercut his writing. By the mid-1960s, Ginsberg's political work would absorb far more of his time than his increasingly diffuse and often-dictated poems, and he would complain to Jane Kramer, his first biographer, that he talked about escaping to the woods to write for a year, and sometimes longed for "the simple, private pleasures of a homey Hindu kirtan or a sacred orgy among friends."** He gave his political energies and his grassroots organizing expertise variously to the Peace Movement, freedom of speech efforts, the fight to legalize marijuana, and a host of progressive causes, such as the dissemination of Buddhist thought in America.

Curiously, while Ginsberg is a gay icon, he was not necessarily considered a gay rights activist by others in the emerging movement. Randy Wicker, a New York activist and media campaigner, knew Ginsberg because they were both part of the five-member League for the Legalization of Marijuana. He credits Ginsberg with being out of the closet in the reactionary 1950s, and with writing *Howl*, "which was certainly liberating. However, he never was involved in the gay liberation movement with the one exception when he picketed the United Nations with me and The Homosexual League of New York protesting Castro's incarceration of homosexuals in 1964."***

* D'Emilio, 181.
** Kramer, 94.
*** Email to the editor of this volume, Dec. 7, 2003.

"Allen wasn't considered a bona fide gay civil rights activist by those of us in the 1960s vanguard of our movement," agrees Jack Nichols, who edited the first gay weekly newspaper in America, *Gay*. But his fame did draw attention to the small but historically pivotal uprising in Greenwich Village that began with a routine police raid of the Stonewall Inn on the night of June 27, 1969. Two nights later, as the street riot was dying down, Ginsberg visited the Stonewall and told a *Village Voice* reporter: "You know, the guys there were so beautiful. They've lost that wounded look that fags all had ten years ago."

Ginsberg's enduring contribution to the gay liberation movement is his visibility as an out gay man, as well as a body of work that celebrates gay male sexuality, from *Howl* to *Straight Hearts' Delight*, a 1980 collection of his queer poems alongside writings by his lover, Peter Orlovsky, to a series of erotic poems on Neal Cassady. He made good use of his bad reputation, too, in coaching Vietnam-era protégés who were hoping to beat the draft: "Tell them you love them, tell them you slept with *me*."

William Burroughs lacked the benevolent public persona of Allen Ginsberg, who could quell riots at poetry festivals by stretching his hands toward the audience and intoning "Ommmm." A gray, spectral figure, dubbed "El Hombre Invisible" by the Spanish hustlers in Tangier, Burroughs dressed like a 1950s narcotics agent or a low-level spy. He was tight-lipped on first meetings, and in Paris practiced a technique of envisioning his visitors back outside his door, in the hallway. Almost always they got up to leave. The most intellectual of the Beat writers, he also believed in possession by evil spirits, thought control, and wish machines. His writings are exuberantly violent, with a strong strain of misogyny alongside his loathing of male effeminacy. In Mexico City in September 1951, he killed Joan Vollmer Burroughs, by then his common-law wife, in a drunken William Tell stunt with a handgun. All these are good reasons for his uneasy position in the gay literary canon. To further complicate appreciation of his work, he had a fully functioning Protestant horror of the flesh: a form of self-disgust that today we might call internalized homophobia if it didn't flatten history into a tasteless wafer.

"Burroughs's work appealed to the alienated," says Ira Silverberg, a longtime friend and the coeditor of *Word Virus*, "whether they were queer or not. His queer audience is the smallest."* Like Ginsberg, he did nothing to ingratiate himself with gay readers in particular. But those on the fringes—much further out than sexual orientation alone could put one—saw his vision as more daring and apocalyptic, both more surreal and, paradoxically, more realistic than either Ginsberg's or Kerouac's. He was the patron saint of junkies. When he rented his windowless basement apartment at 222 Bowery ("The Bunker") in New York City in 1974, he learned there was a neighborhood drug dealer with the street name "Doctor Nova," after his novel *Nova Express*. And though his thinking was progressive on many issues, like the 1980s "War on Drugs" and the environment, he was no kitten with respect to gun control or other "socialist" tendencies in government. Perhaps because, unlike Ginsberg, Burroughs didn't embody a unified set of values, his impact on pop culture was still on the rise when the youth culture faded into the conservative 1980s. His later influence on gay liberation was oblique, coming through his refusal to succumb to the taming forces of the marketplace and his depictions of fantasy worlds in which gay sex and male–male bonding were less the exceptions than the rule.

Although the quest for authenticity led the Beat writers in different directions formally and thematically, their work shares a queer tension between violence and gentleness, between contrasting models of masculinity, between primitive faith and rational suspicion. In their lives as well as in their writings, they maintained porous boundaries between male camaraderie and sexual desire. There is a violent and self-destructive aspect to their physical indulgences: Kerouac was a cantankerous drunk who eventually killed himself with alcohol; Cassady died of exposure in

* Conversation with the editor of this volume, November 2003.

Mexico in 1968 after mixing downers and alcohol; Burroughs shot his wife, alienated his alcoholic son, and lost many productive years to his drug addictions. But at its best, the Beat legacy is one of celebration, tenderness, sincerity, and spontaneity in life as in art. "There's no doubt," said Burroughs, "that we're living in a freer America as a result of the Beat literary movement, which is an important part of the larger picture of cultural and political change in this country during the last forty years, when a four-letter word couldn't appear on the printed page, and minority rights were ridiculous."*

Queer Beats: How the Beats Turned America On to Sex brings together a diverse collection of primary and secondary texts that allow the Beat writers to be viewed from and through the perspective of their fluid sexuality. It is the first book of its nature. There is, of course, more queer and queer-ish Beats writing than could be included in any single volume, but I hope that *Queer Beats* provides a starting point for further reading and fresh insights.**

The three sections—The Road of Excess (Or, Saintly Sinners), Male Muses (Or, Sex without Borders), and Queer Shoulder to the Wheel—were originally conceived of as chronological, though this proved far too rigid a plan. Nevertheless, I've tried to pursue narrative threads where they occur. Emphasis is on the three principal Beats—Kerouac, Ginsberg, and Burroughs—together with their friends and lovers, but I include contributions by related figures on the queer Beat fringe, like Paul and Jane Bowles; gay poets John Wieners, Alan Ansen, and Harold Norse; Diane di Prima (though her bisexuality doesn't figure in the orgy scene from *Memoirs of a Beatnik* included here); and poet/performer John Giorno, famous for founding Dial-a-Poem, starring in Andy Warhol's first film, *Sleep*, and, in a post-Beat gesture of gratuitous candor,

---

* Quoted in Anne Waldman's *The Beat Book* (New York: Random House, 1996).
** Jamie Russell's excellent *Queer Burroughs* (London: Palgrave, 2001) was the first book-length study of an individual Beat writer's sexuality, and of its influence on his work and his critical reception.

publishing the cock sizes of the writers and artists he'd had sex with. One of Giorno's contributions here, "I Met Jack Kerouac For One Glorious Moment in 1958…," comes from his unpublished memoir-in-progress.

In the spirit of the Beats, I've preserved all instances of unconventional spelling or grammar in the originals.

Regina Marler
San Francisco
April 2004

I.

The Road of Excess

(Or, Saintly Sinners)

Advice for young artists is hopelessly contradictory, but almost no one would propose the kind of Dionysian abandon that the Beat writers relished in the early days of their friendship—on the streets and in the bars of New York City (fabled places like the San Remo, the West End Bar, the Cedar Street Tavern), and then on the various stops on the Beat circuit: Denver, San Francisco, Mexico City, Tangier, Paris. "The only people for me are the mad ones," wrote Kerouac in the most famous lines of that ode to excess, *On the Road*, "the ones who are mad to live, mad to talk, mad to be saved, desirous of everything at the same time, the ones who never yawn or say a commonplace thing, but burn, burn, burn..."*

"Mad" behavior was essential to the Beats, their first answer to the conformist ethos of the 1940s and 1950s. They cultivated—and applauded—a lack of inhibition: sex at a moment's notice, with a hustler or a friend or a friend's lover; sudden arrivals and departures; big arguments and reconciliations. To quiet a heckler at a Los Angeles poetry reading in 1957, Ginsberg stripped off his clothes. Their writing methods came to reflect their philosophies of life, with both Ginsberg and Kerouac adopting the Buddhist motto "First thought, best thought" as an argument for leaving their hastily written first drafts untouched. In "The Essentials of Spontaneous Prose," Kerouac advocated writing in a semitrance—like a jazz improvisation—and not allowing the conscious mind to censor after the fact. The rhythms should be free, following the

* *On the Road*, 9.

3

breath and natural speech patterns. Punctuation was a straitjacket. A dash here and there would do. Nothing should be allowed to slow the flow of the authentic: "the best writing is always the most painful personal wrung-out tossed from cradle warm protective mind-tap from yourself."

Luckily, Ginsberg and Kerouac were able to write while high, since they pursued, like Rimbaud, a systematic derangement of the senses. Even a dose of nitrous oxide at the dentist's office could send Ginsberg into a state of "explicit Nirvana." Dreams, visions, and drug trances could be equally inspiring. In November 1958, Ginsberg composed fifty-eight pages of his elegy for his mother, "Kaddish," in a forty-hour burst, fueled by injections of heroin and liquid Methedrine, with the occasional Dexedrine tablet.*

In the panicked era of *Reefer Madness*, the Beats were amazingly sanguine about what they put into their bodies. There was little they wouldn't try. An acquaintance once saw Joan Burroughs's purse fall open on the floor. Pills of every color and shape spilled out. "There was a mystery about drugs," wrote Michael McClure in *Scratching the Beat Surface*, "and they were taken for joy, for consciousness, for spiritual elevation, or for what the Romantic poet Keats called 'Soul-making.' " Like their fluid sexuality, drug use was crucial to their work and their relationships, and fueled the constant crossing of boundaries that characterizes Beat writing. Both Ginsberg and Burroughs went as far as the Peruvian jungle to experience the hallucinogen *yage* (*ayahuasca*), a quest recounted in their book, *The Yage Letters*. When Timothy Leary began his investigations into LSD at Harvard University, Ginsberg was quick to volunteer. At a Senate Judiciary Subcommittee on narcotics legislation in spring 1966, Ginsberg suggested that the senators look on acid as a "useful educational tool." He described for them his peyote visions, and how *yage* helped him loosen up about women.

---

* A contradictory blend, since heroin is a narcotic and Methedrine and Dexedrine are amphetamines (speed).

William Burroughs's list was the most impressive. The opiates alone included "opium, smoked and taken orally, [...] heroin injected in the skin, vein, muscle, sniffed (when no needle was available), morphine, dilaudid, pantopon, eukadol, paracodeine, dionine, codeine, demerol, methadone." In Paris, Gregory Corso saw Burroughs fixing and asked if he could try it, as well. Soon Corso was addicted to "the white muse" and joined Burroughs in his daily attempts to score. Although Burroughs's first novel was the narcotic autobiography *Junky* (1953), he didn't write well on junk. In the grip of addiction, he would lock himself in his rented room and stare at his toes for weeks. Sometimes he would pay friends to execute "reduction cures," hiding his clothes, policing the door, and doling out decreasing doses of his current habit to the naked, drug-sick patient. "You become a narcotics addict because you do not have strong motivations in any other direction," Burroughs told an interviewer for *Heroin Times*. "Junk wins by default."

In the 1960s, Burroughs informed a *Paris Review* interviewer that opiates were no help in writing, though marijuana had its uses. He tried to grow some at his New Waverley, Texas, farm in 1947, but the poorly cured product fetched almost nothing when he sold it in New York. The Beats used marijuana much as their Tangier friend Paul Bowles relied on *majoun*—not only as a key to the unconscious, but also as a gentle, daily adjustment to sobriety. The poster of Ginsberg marching in Sheridan Square wearing a homemade "Pot Is Fun" sign was ubiquitous in hippie households of the 1960s. Neal Cassady was the Johnny Appleseed of cannibis, distributing joints wherever he went. Kerouac became such an enthusiast that he declared, "War will be impossible when marijuana becomes legal."* Although always a quick writer, Kerouac lavished a full three weeks in July 1952 on the experimental *Dr. Sax*, puffing weed

---

* *Visions of Cody*, 300. A dedicated tea-head, Neal Cassady eventually served two years in San Quentin for trying to barter a couple of joints to two undercover policemen for a ride to work. The judge had not been moved when someone told him that Cassady was the hero of *On the Road*.

around the clock. The novel's loose, rolling, sex-steeped prose (which one biographer called "a madly sensible gibberish") is evidence not only of his constant buzz, but of the Mexico City brothels he was frequenting for 36 cents a toss.

But before the romance of marijuana, there was the Benzedrine Inhaler, patented in 1932, which comes up so often in Beat memoirs that it is almost a minor character. A highly addictive treatment for asthma, Benzedrine came in the form of accordion-pleated, amphetamine-soaked papers tucked into a small vial. When Herbert Huncke couldn't afford junk, he stumbled around Times Square in a Benzedrine haze. Joan Burroughs and Jack Kerouac, in what Kerouac would later call "a year of low, evil decadence" at their West 115th Street apartment, would crumple the papers into little balls and drop them into cups of coffee or Coke for a jittery all-day high. Kerouac wrote *The Subterraneans* on a three-day Benzedrine rush. Perhaps because he had the outlet of his writing, he seemed to handle the drug better than Joan Burroughs, who hallucinated a violent marriage for her downstairs neighbors, and once, in a panic, sent Ginsberg and Kerouac downstairs to break up a fight. They found the apartment empty.*

Had William Burroughs been a different sort of husband, he might have objected to Joan's drug use, especially during her pregnancy with their son, Billy. But while Burroughs took his financial responsibilities as a family man very seriously, his marriage to Joan was an alliance of addicts. Only once did he hit her. Frustrated to see him back on junk, she had knocked a spoonful out of his hand. No one in the circle was sure how the enthusiastically straight Joan worked out her sexual relationship with Burroughs, but a few years later, when Ginsberg confronted him about his buying boys in Mexico when he was married to Joan, Burroughs snapped: "I never made any pretensions of permanent heterosexual

---

* In today's parlance, Joan Burroughs was a speed freak, which puts into perspective her single-minded pursuit of altered states.

orientation. [...] Nor are we in any particular mess. There is, of course, as there was from the beginning, an impasse, and cross purposes that are, in all likelihood, not amenable to any solution."* Part of their arrangement seems to have been that Joan would not pressure Burroughs emotionally. A visitor to their Texas farm recalled Joan tapping on Bill's door one night and asking if she could just lie in his arms for a while.

Joan devised a parenting philosophy of genial neglect, which allowed her to spend most of every day drunk or high. By 1951, the year of her death, she was walking with a limp from untreated polio. Her teeth had been blackened by drug use, and she had open sores on her arms. Unable to get Benzedrine in Mexico, she had switched to tequila, which she sipped all day. Lucien Carr and Allen Ginsberg visited her a few days before her death, while Burroughs was away with his boyfriend Lewis Marker. She took them on a wild, high-speed drive to Guadalajara to meet a pot connection. Both Lucien and Joan were drunk. Sometimes she steered while he lay on the floor working the gas pedal. A terrified Ginsberg cowered in the backseat with Joan's children, shouting for her to stop. Joan's death wish was obvious to Ginsberg. She was twenty-seven. A few days later at an acquaintance's apartment, her husband, aiming his pistol an inch above the glass balanced on her head, shot her in the forehead from six feet away.

In "The Death of Joan," Burroughs's biographer and literary executor, James Grauerholz, has reconstructed the event from the standpoint of each witness. There's no evidence that Joan's shooting was anything but a drunken stunt gone awry. But for the rest of his life, Burroughs would believe he had been possessed by evil at that moment, or that in some awful way Joan's brain had drawn the bullet toward it. Whatever her role—psychic or otherwise—in the shooting, Joan's decline and death were among the bitter consequences of the revelry that had begun so innocently in the mid-1940s. In a sense, she was the third casualty of

* Quoted in Miles, 51.

the Beat search for supreme reality.* As much as *Howl* is a celebration of excess—of crazy sex, drugs, self-assertion—it is also a lament for those, like her, who did not survive the times.

* After Dave Kammerer, there was the prankster Bill Cannastra, a queer friend of the Beats who died in October 1950. See Alan Ansen's "Dead Drunk," included here.

Allen Ginsberg

In Society

I walked into the cocktail party
room and found three or four queers
talking together in queertalk.
I tried to be friendly but heard
myself talking to one in hiptalk.
"I'm glad to see you," he said, and
looked away. "Hmn," I mused. The room
was small and had a double-decker
bed in it, and cooking apparatus:
icebox, cabinet, toasters, stove;
the hosts seemed to live with room
enough only for cooking and sleeping.
My remark on this score was understood but not appreciated. I was
offered refreshments, which I accepted.
I ate a sandwich of pure meat; an
enormous sandwich of human flesh,
I noticed, while I was chewing on it,
it also included a dirty asshole.

More company came, including a
fluffy female who looked like
a princess. She glared at me and
said immediately: "I don't like you,"
turned her head away, and refused
to be introduced. I said, "What!"
in outrage. "Why you shit-faced fool!"

This got everybody's attention.
"Why you narcissistic bitch! How
can you decide when you don't even
know me," I continued in a violent
and messianic voice, inspired at
last, dominating the whole room.

1947

Herbert Huncke

On Meeting Kinsey

One afternoon when I was sitting in Chase's cafeteria I was approached by a young girl who asked if she could join me. She was carrying several books in her arms and was obviously a student. "There's someone who wants to meet you," she told me.

I said, "Yes, who?"

"A Professor Kinsey."

I had never heard of him and she went on to say, "Well, he's a professor at Indiana University and he's doing research on sex. He is requesting people to talk about their sex lives, and to be as honest about it as possible."

My immediate reaction was that there was some very strange character in the offing who was too shy to approach people himself, someone who probably had some very weird sex kick and was using this girl to pander for him. But I sounded her down.

She must have known what the score was insofar as sex, but I didn't know that. I didn't want to shock her, but at the same time I wanted to find out exactly what the story was, so I questioned her rather closely about this man. I asked her why he hadn't approached me himself, and she said, "He felt it would be better if someone else spoke with you. He has seen you around, and he thought you might be very interesting to talk to. I'll tell you what I'll do. I'll give you his name and number." At that time he was staying in a very nice East Side hotel. "You can call him and discuss the situation with him."

I had nothing else to do, and I said, "Well, I might as well find out what this is all about."

I called Kinsey and he said, "Oh, yes, I'd like to speak with you very much."

"What exactly is it you're interested in?" I asked him.

"All I want you to do," he said to me, "is tell me about your sex life, what experiences you've had, what your interests are, whether you've masturbated and how often, whether you've had any homosexual experiences."

"That all you want?" I said.

"That's all I want."

"Well, I think it's only fair to tell you," I went on, "and I don't want to be crude—but I do need money."

He said, "I'd certainly be willing to give you some money. Would ten dollars be all right?"

"It certainly would."

We went through a funny exchange. Kinsey wanted me to come up to his place, and I said, "No, I'd rather not do that. I'd rather meet you somewhere first." I did not trust him yet. There was just something about the whole thing that sounded very offbeat to me. I arranged to have him meet me at a bar. "I'll meet you at the bar, but I don't drink," he said. "But I'll buy you a drink."

"All right, fair enough."

"I'll know you when I see you," he told me, "so you sit down and order yourself a drink and I'll be there in a while." We were to meet at a popular bar on [Times] Square [...]

I didn't have enough money to buy myself a drink, and I sort of kicked around in front of the place until I saw a cab pull up and a man get out. Kinsey had a very interesting appearance, strictly professorial. His hair was cut very short, slightly gray. He had a round face that was pleasant appearing, and he was dressed in a suit—obviously a conservative man, I thought.

He walked up to me and said, "I'm Kinsey. You're Herbert Huncke. Let's go in. You'd like to have a drink."

I said, "Yes, I'd like to talk to you a few moments before we go to your hotel." He again gave me much the same story the girl had, and he assured me that the only thing he was interested in was the discussion, though he did say he wanted to measure the size of the penis. He showed me a card which had a phallus drawn on it. He said he'd like to know the length of it when erect and when soft. Naturally, I was wondering when he was going to get to the point. It was all so strange, and I still did not quite believe him, but I thought, Well, hell, I might just as well go along with him and see what it's all about.

As it turned out, it was a very delightful experience. As I started rapping to Kinsey about my sex life, I sort of unburdened myself of many things that I'd long been keeping to myself. For example, I'd always masturbated, all the way up until I kind of lost interest in sex altogether around the age of fifty. When I told others of my confessions to Kinsey they all said I was off my rocker, but I must say I was thankful by that time to get it out of my system. Sex had always played a prominent role in my life. I earned my living from sex at one time and have met all kinds of people, and heard of and had experiences with some very strange fetishes.

I told Kinsey most of these things. In *Huncke's Journal* I describe an interesting experience I had as a young boy, and I spoke to him about this. It tells of a young fellow, about twenty years old, who, after telling me dirty stories and arousing me with pornographic pictures, suggested we go up into a building together. We did, and he suddenly startled me by dropping his pants. There he was with an erection. This thing looked gigantic to me, being eight or nine years old, because it just happened that it was dead in front of my face. I drew back but at the same time I say in all honesty that I was somehow interested. I felt no fear.

He said he wanted to feel me. I was embarrassed. Here was my tiny hunk of flesh and then this gigantic thing standing in front of me. It didn't seem right somehow. Anyway, he did try and convince me that it would be a good idea if I'd allow him to put it up my rectum. I certainly drew the line at that, because I knew it'd be very painful. I assured him I wasn't about to cooperate, and he didn't press the issue. He proceeded to masturbate furiously and then he ejaculated. That was my first experience with anyone other than children my own age. This was the first thing I thought of when I began to masturbate. It would excite me. Instead of following the normal course and being pleased by visions of a little girl, I was attracted to this big phallus—a cock. It was quite an experience. I had never told anyone about it until I told Kinsey. It was this sort of thing that I unburdened myself of to this man.

As I continued to speak to him, he became so adept at his questioning and his approach that there was no embarrassment on my part, and I found myself relaxing. The one thing I could not supply him with was a size to my penis. He finally gave me a card and asked me to fill it out and send it to him later on, which, incidentally, I never did.*

---

* Huncke did several more interviews with Kinsey, and afterward gathered two-dollar referral fees for sending his friends and acquaintances to speak with the doctor. In this way, Burroughs, Ginsberg, and Joan Vollmer Burroughs came to be interviewed by Kinsey.

William S. Burroughs

"Nobler, I thought, to die a man than live on, a sex monster..."

from QUEER

Lee and Allerton went to see Cocteau's *Orpheus*. In the dark theater Lee could feel his body pull towards Allerton, an amoeboid protoplasmic projection, straining with a blind worm hunger to enter the other's body, to breathe with his lungs, see with his eyes, learn the feel of his viscera and genitals. Allerton shifted in his seat. Lee felt a sharp twinge, a strain or dislocation of the spirit. His eyes ached. He took off his glasses and ran his hand over his closed eyes.

When they left the theater, Lee felt exhausted. He fumbled and bumped into things. His voice was toneless with strain. He put his hand up to his head from time to time, an awkward, involuntary gesture of pain. "I need a drink," he said. He pointed to a bar across the street. "There," he said.

He sat down in a booth and ordered a double tequila. Allerton ordered rum and Coke. Lee drank the tequila straight down, listening down into himself for the effect. He ordered another.

"What did you think of the picture?" Lee asked.

"Enjoyed parts of it."

"Yes." Lee nodded, pursing his lips and looking down into his empty glass. "So did I." He pronounced the words very carefully, like an elocution teacher.

"He always gets some innaresting effects." Lee laughed. Euphoria was spreading from his stomach. He drank half the second tequila. "The innaresting thing about Cocteau is his ability to bring the myth alive in modern terms."

"Ain't it the truth?" said Allerton.

—

15

They went to a Russian restaurant for dinner. Lee looked through the menu. "By the way," he said, "the law was in putting the bite on the Ship Ahoy [a bar] again. Vice Squad. Two hundred pesos. I can see them in the station house after a hard day shaking down citizens of the Federal District. One cop says, 'Ah, Gonzalez, you should see what I got today. Oh la la, such a bite!'

" 'Aah, you shook down a *puto* queer for two *pesetas* in a bus station crapper. We know you, Hernandez, and your cheap tricks. You're the cheapest cop inna Federal District.' "

Lee waved to the waiter. "Hey, Jack. *Dos* martinis, much dry. *Seco.* And *dos* plates Sheeska Babe. *Sabe?*"

The waiter nodded. "That's two dry martinis and two orders of shish kebab. Right, gentlemen?"

"Solid, Pops.... So how was your evening with Dumé?"

"We went to several bars full of queers. One place a character asked me to dance and propositioned me."

"Take him up?"

"No."

"Dumé is a nice fellow."

Allerton smiled. "Yes, but he is not a person I would confide too much in. That is, anything I wanted to keep private."

"You refer to a specific indiscretion?"

"Frankly, yes."

"I see." Lee thought, "Dume never misses."

The waiter put two martinis on the table. Lee held his martini up to the candle, looking at it with distaste. "The inevitable watery martini with a decomposing olive," he said.

Lee bought a lottery ticket from a boy of ten or so, who had rushed in when the waiter went to the kitchen. The boy was working the last-ticket routine. Lee paid him expansively, like a drunk American. "Go buy yourself some marijuana, son," he said. The boy smiled and turned to leave. "Come back in five years and make an easy ten pesos," Lee called after him.

—

16

Allerton smiled. "Thank god," Lee thought. "I won't have to contend with middle-class morality."

"Here you are, sir," said the waiter, placing the shish kebab on the table.

Lee ordered two glasses of red wine. "So Dumé told you about my, uh, proclivities?" he said abruptly.

"Yes," said Allerton, his mouth full.

"A curse. Been in our family for generations. The Lees have always been perverts. I shall never forget the unspeakable horror that froze the lymph in my glands—the lymph glands that is, of course—when the baneful word seared my reeling brain: *I was a homosexual.* I thought of the painted, simpering female impersonators I had seen in a Baltimore night club. Could I be one of those subhuman things? I walked the streets in a daze, like a man with a light concussion—just a minute, Doctor Kildare, this isn't your script. I might well have destroyed myself, ending an existence which seemed to offer nothing but grotesque misery and humiliation. Nobler, I thought, to die a man than live on, a sex monster. It was a wise old queen—Bobo, we called her—who taught me that I had a duty to live and to bear my burden proudly for all to see, to conquer prejudice and ignorance and hate with knowledge and sincerity and love. Whenever you are threatened by a hostile presence, you emit a thick cloud of love like an octopus squirts out ink...

"Poor Bobo came to a sticky end. He was riding in the Duc de Ventre's Hispano-Suiza when his falling piles blew out of the car and wrapped around the rear wheel. He was completely gutted, leaving an empty shell sitting there on the giraffe-skin upholstery. Even the eyes and the brain went, with a horrible shlupping sound. The Duc says he will carry that ghastly shlup with him to his mausoleum....

"Then I knew the meaning of loneliness. But Bobo's words came back to me from the tomb, the sibilants cracking gently. 'No one is ever really alone. You are part of everything alive.' The difficulty is to convince someone else he is really part of you, so what the hell? Us parts ought to work together. Reet?"

Lee paused, looking at Allerton speculatively. "Just where do I stand with the kid?" he wondered. He had listened politely, smiling at intervals. "What I mean is, Allerton, we are all parts of a tremendous whole. No use fighting it." Lee was getting tired of the routine. He looked around restlessly for some place to put it down. "Don't these gay bars depress you? Of course, the queer bars here aren't to compare with Stateside queer joints."

"I wouldn't know," said Allerton. "I've never been in any queer joints except those Dumé took me to. I guess there's kicks and kicks."

"You haven't, really?"

"No, never."

Lee paid the bill and they walked out into the cool night. A crescent moon was clear and green in the sky. They walked aimlessly.

"Shall we go to my place for a drink? I have some Napoleon brandy."

"All right," said Allerton.

"This is a completely unpretentious little brandy, you understand, none of this tourist treacle with obvious effects of flavoring, appealing to the mass tongue. My brandy has no need of shoddy devices to shock and coerce the palate. Come along." Lee called a cab.

"Three pesos to Insurgentes and Monterrey," Lee said to the driver in his atrocious Spanish. The driver said four. Lee waved him on. The driver muttered something, and opened the door.

Inside, Lee turned to Allerton. "The man plainly harbors subversive thoughts. You know, when I was at Princeton, Communism was the thing. To come out flat for private property and a class society, you marked yourself a stupid lout or suspect to be a High Episcopalian pederast. But I held out against the infection—of Communism I mean, of course."

"Aqui." Lee handed three pesos to the driver, who muttered some more and started the car with a vicious class of gears.

"Sometimes I think they don't like us," said Allerton.

"I don't mind people disliking me," Lee said. "The question is, what are they in a position to do about it? Apparently nothing, at present.

They don't have the green light. This driver, for example, hates gringos. But if he kills someone—and very possibly he will—it will not be an American. It will be another Mexican. Maybe his good friend. Friends are less frightening than strangers."

Lee opened the door of his apartment and turned on the light. The apartment was pervaded by seemingly hopeless disorder. Here and there, ineffectual attempts had been made to arrange things in piles. There were no lived-in touches. No pictures, no decorations. Clearly, none of the furniture was his. But Lee's presence permeated the apartment. A coat over the back of a chair and a hat on the table were immediately recognizable as belonging to Lee.

"I'll fix you a drink." Lee got two water glasses from the kitchen and poured two inches of Mexican brandy in each glass.

Allerton tasted the brandy. "Good Lord," he said. "Napoleon must have pissed in this one."

"I was afraid of that. An untutored palate. Your generation has never learned the pleasures that a trained palate confers on the disciplined few."

Lee took a long drink of the brandy. He attempted an ecstatic "aah," inhaled some of the brandy, and began to cough. "It *is* god-awful," he said when he could talk. "Still, better than California brandy. It has a suggestion of cognac taste."

There was a long silence. Allerton was sitting with his head leaned back against the couch. His eyes were half closed.

"Can I show you over the house?" said Lee, standing up. "In here we have the bedroom."

Allerton got to his feet slowly. They went into the bedroom, and Allerton lay down on the bed and lit a cigarette. Lee sat in the only chair.

"More brandy?" Lee asked. Allerton nodded. Lee sat down on the edge of the bed, and filled his glass and handed it to him. Lee touched his sweater. "Sweet stuff, dearie," he said. "That wasn't made in Mexico."

"I bought it in Scotland," he said. He began to hiccough violently, and got up and rushed for the bathroom.

Lee stood in the doorway. "Too bad," he said. "What could be the matter? You didn't drink too much." He filled a glass with water and handed it to Allerton. "You all right now?" he asked.

"Yes, I think so." Allerton lay down on the bed again.

Lee reached out a hand and touched Allerton's ear, and caressed the side of his face. Allerton reached up and covered one of Lee's hands and squeezed it.

"Let's get this sweater off."

"O.K.," said Allerton. He took off his sweater and then lay down again. Lee took off his own shoes and shirt. He opened Allerton's shirt and ran his hand down Allerton's ribs and stomach, which contracted beneath his fingers. "God, you're skinny," he said.

"I'm pretty small."

Lee took off Allerton's shoes and socks. He loosened Allerton's belt and unbuttoned his trousers. Allerton arched his body, and Lee pulled the trousers and drawers off. He dropped his own trousers and shorts and lay down beside him. Allerton responded without hostility or disgust, but in his eyes Lee saw a curious detachment, the impersonal calm of an animal or a child.

Later, when they lay side by side smoking, Lee said, "Oh, by the way, you said you had a camera in pawn that you were about to lose?" It occurred to Lee that to bring the matter up at this time was not tactful, but he decided the other was not the type to take offense.

"Yes. In for four hundred pesos. The ticket runs out next Wednesday."

"Well, let's go down tomorrow and get it out."

Allerton raised one bare shoulder off the sheet. "O.K.," he said.

Alan Ansen

Dead Drunk

In Memoriam
William Cannastra
1924-1950

For Winifred Gregoire

[Joan Burroughs was not the only member of the group to reach a violent end. There was, of course, Dave Kammerer, stabbed to death by Lucien Carr. Less well known was Bill Cannastra, a Harvard Law School graduate and queer prankster famous for heavy drinking and public stunts like running around the block naked. Cannastra had been trying to go straight when he died, having drunkenly attempted to climb out a subway window as it left the Bleecker Street station. A month later, in November 1950, Kerouac married Cannastra's girlfriend, Joan Haverty.

It was in memory of Cannastra that Alan Ansen, perhaps the best "undiscovered" Beat poet, wrote "Dead Drunk." Ansen was a friend to the Beats and secretary to W. H. Auden. Much of his openly gay poetry was published privately and distributed to friends, as James Merrill wrote, "at his own caprice." Ansen is Rollo Greb in *On the Road* and A. J. in William Burroughs's *Naked Lunch*. In Tangier, he and Ginsberg worked six-hour days for two months to pull the manuscript of Burroughs's *Naked Lunch* into shape. Ansen's late collection *Contact Highs* (1989) was praised by Ginsberg for its "lunatic personal genius."—ed.]

1

And the muddy glasses on the floor stinking of stale beer and smelly
    red wine
And the wreath of crisp dead ivy decorating the loft floor grave
And the senile remains of a rice and lamb hearts casserole on top of the
    great rusty stove
And a welter of theologians and script girls on the huge triple bed in
    the coma that confounds the just and the apathetic
And the garbage man sleeping alone on a little truckle bed in the corner
And the hum of the hi-fi nobody remembered to switch off
And the smashed Victrola record sprawling helpless at the feet of many
    accusing intact albums
And the indefatigable book review sucking a spent athlete on an
    off-centre divan
And the eyeglasses the empty bottles the books the draughtsman's tools
    the blank sheets of paper the dead letters
And the host supine staring brown-eyed at the Everest ceiling of his
overtenanted loft.

2

But once the ivy lived
Wrapping the warm brown naked body in tendrils of vivacious green
As it danced through gray and hostile streets
Joy to the world or at least
The moment's festivity,
Pan.

For pipes a gramophone,
Glasses for hoofs keynote a face that entices all the others' need
To be tender, hot, expansive to
Giveless mirages that crave

And crave in a vacuum
Graves.

Wild the gestures, liquid muscles, rippling eyes and a voice that is so
    alone with you in a room that sometimes even you aren't there;
But all in vain.
The great god Pan is dead.

3

Let the sluices and sloshes of goblets and bottles lap high,
Let the air
Churn and gurgle with waves of poured liquids and vinous good feeling
As we reeling
From one bar to another in search of a brother get lost
In an early fall frost.
For in spite of our prancing and Corybant dancing as lamsters from
    care
The trains rattle by
And the choleric sky
As we lean out the moving subway car's window
Toward the iron stanchion and its splattered future of our blobs of
    blood and brain
Has decreed and glaring still decrees that we die.

Herbert Huncke

Youth

When I was a schoolboy—age fifteen—living In what was conceded to be a respectable middle-class neighborhood in Chicago—I had my first encounter with love.

In the apartment building in which I lived with my mother, brother and grandmother (my mother and father had been divorced two years previously), there were several women who owned Chow dogs and they would pay me to take their dogs out for walks. This afforded me opportunity to make something of a show of myself—since Chows were quite fashionable—and as I considered myself at least personable in appearance, it rather pleased me to imagine that people seeing me walking along the Drive must surely think me the owner and certainly attractive with my pet straining at the leash. Frequently I would walk one of the dogs late in the evening and it was on such an occasion I first met Dick.

I had decided before returning home to stop by the neighborhood drugstore and as I was leaving someone spoke my name. I looked into the most piercing brown—almost black brown—eyes I had ever seen. They belonged to a man who at the time was in his late twenties—fairly well built—not too tall—with somewhat aquiline features and exceedingly black hair which he wore combed flat to his head. I learned later he was of Russian Jewish parentage.

I was very much impressed by his appearance and felt a strange sensation upon first seeing him which was to be repeated each time we met for as long as I knew him. I never quite got over a certain physical response to his personality and even now in retrospect I find myself conscious of an inner warmth.

As I was leaving the drugstore and after he had spoken my name and I had smiled and flushed, he commented that I didn't know him but that a friend of his had spoken with me one evening about my dog and that I had given him my name, and he in turn had given it to him when they had seen me walking and he had asked if his friend noticed me. He then asked me if I would object to his accompanying me home so that we might become better acquainted. He gave me to understand that he wanted to know me. I was no end pleased by his attention and became animated and flirtatious.

We had a thoroughly enjoyable walk and from that point on I began seeing him fairly regularly. He was in the recording business and second in charge of a floor of recording studios in one of the large well-known buildings off Lake Shore Drive a short distance north of the Loop. He knew innumerable people in show business and I spent as much time hanging around the studio as could be arranged. Sometimes we would lunch together or stay downtown for dinner or go to a movie or he would take me along while he interviewed some possible recording star, and it was after some such instance at the old Sherman Hotel that he suggested since it was late I call home and ask permission to spend the night downtown. This I was anxious to do as I had long had the desire to sleep with him.

I was still rather green as to what was expected in a homosexual relationship, but I did know I was exceedingly desirous of feeling his body near mine and was sure I could be ingenious enough sexually to make him happy with me.

Actually I had but little experience other than mutual masturbation with others of my own age, and although I knew the word homosexual I wasn't exactly aware of the connotations.

We spent the night together and I discovered that in fact he was nearly as ignorant as I and besides was filled with all sorts of feelings of guilt. We kissed and explored each other's bodies and after both ejaculating fell asleep in each other's arms.

This began a long period in which he professed deep love for me and on one occasion threatened to throw acid in my face should he ever discover me with someone else.

—

The affair followed the usual pattern such affairs follow and after the novelty wore off I became somewhat bored, although it appeased my vanity to feel I had someone so completely in my control. Had anyone threatened my supremacy I would have gone to great lengths to eliminate them from the situation.

About this time it was necessary for him to make a business trip to New York, and when he returned he was wearing a Persian sapphire ring which he explained he would give to me if I would promise to stay away from some of the people and places I had lately been visiting. I promised to do this and considered the ring mine.

One evening we had dinner in a little French restaurant we frequented, and, while eating, a very handsome young man joined us whom Dick introduced as Richard, who was attending classes at the University of Chicago and was someone he had met recently thru some mutual acquaintance. We sat talking and suddenly I was startled to see the ring on Richard's finger.

Richard was considerably younger than Dick and really very beautiful. He was blond, with icy blue eyes—innocent and clear. He was very interested in life and people and kept bombarding us with questions—about our interests, the theater, music, art, or whatever happened to pop into his head. He laughed a good deal and one could feel a sense of goodness about him. He was obviously attracted to me and asked permission to call me on the phone so that we might make arrangements to see each other. I complied and began making plans about how to get the ring away from him—after all I felt the ring was mine—and I wanted it.

And so it happened that I succeeded in twisting one of the few really wondering things that occurred when I was young into a sordid, almost tragic experience which even now fills me with shame.

As I have already said—Richard was good. There was no guile in his makeup and he offered his love and friendship unstintingly. It was he who first introduced me to poetry—to great music—to the beauty of the world—and who was concerned with my wants and happiness. Who spent hours making love to me, caressing and kissing me on every part of my body until I would collapse in a great explosion of beauty and sensation which I have never attained in exactly the same way with anyone since. He truly loved me and asked nothing in return but that I accept him—instead of which I delighted in hurting him and making him suffer in all manner of petty ways. I would tease him or refuse him sex or call him a fool or say that I didn't want to see him. Sometimes I would tell him we were finished, thru, and not to call me or try and see me, and it was after one such episode on a beautiful warm summer night—when I had agreed to see him again if he would grant me a favor—I asked for the ring and he gave it to me.

The next day I visited Dick at the studios and—with many gestures and words of denunciation—flung the ring at him, telling him that we were finished and that anyway he wasn't nearly as amusing as Richard—and that maybe or maybe not I'd continue seeing Richard—and that in fact he bored me and I only felt sorry for him—and that I would never be as big a fool over anyone as he was over me—and besides my only reason for knowing him at all was so that I could get the ring.

Dick became enraged and began calling me foul names which he sort of spit at me and pulled from his desk drawer a pistol. He was waving it in front of my face and at the same time telling me how cruel and heartless I was and that he could forgive the stupidity of my actions in regard to himself but that the harm I was inflicting on Richard was more than he could stomach and I would be better dead. Suddenly he started shouting— "Get out—get out—I never want to see you again." By this time I was shaking and almost unable to stand and stumbled out of his presence.

The following day in the mail I received a letter from Richard containing a poem—that read almost like this—

A perfect fool you called me.
Perchance not as happy in my
    outlook on life and people
    as you—
Yet in like manner—playing the
    role of a perfect fool—
Gave me a sort of bliss—
You in all your wisdom—will
    never know.

Shortly after receiving the letter I called Richard and asked to see him. He refused to see me and at that time I would not plead. A strange thing had happened to me—I had become aware—almost overnight— of the enormity of my cruelty—and I was filled with a sudden sense of loneliness—which I have never lost—and I wanted Richard's forgiveness.

Richard never forgave me and I have only seen him once since the time he gave me the ring—and that was only long enough for him to tell me—he was trying to forget he had known me.

It was a cold winter day.

Nor did I ever speak with Dick again. Not so many years ago—I read in the paper—he is dead.

1959

William Burroughs

"I don't mind being called queer..."

from a letter to Allen Ginsberg, April 22, 1952

[The publishers of *Junkie* had requested a biographical preface from Burroughs. Ginsberg was serving as Burroughs's agent, and had sold the manuscript to his friend Carl Solomon at Ace Books.—ed.]

Now as to this biographical thing, I can't write it. It is too general and I have no idea what they want. Do they have in mind the—"I have worked (but not in the order named) as towel boy in a Kalamazoo whore house, lavatory attendant, male whore and part-time stool pigeon. Currently living in a remodelled pissoir with a hermaphrodite and a succession of cats. I would rather write than fuck (what a shameless lie). My principal hobby is torturing the cats—we have quite a turnover. Especially in Siameses. That long silky hair cries aloud for kerosene and a match. I favor kerosene over gasoline. It burns *slower*. You'd be surprised at the noises a cat can make when the chips are down"—routine, like you see on the back flap? Please, Sweetheart, write the fucking thing will you? PLUMMM. That's a great big sluppy kiss for my favorite agent. Now look, you tell Solomon I don't mind being called queer. T. E. Lawrence and all manner of right Joes (boy can I turn a phrase) was queer. But I'll see him castrated before I'll be called a Fag. That's just what I been trying to put down uh I mean *over*, is the distinction between us strong, manly, noble types and the leaping, jumping, window dressing cocksucker. Furthecrissakes a girl's gotta draw the line somewheres or publishers will swarm all over her sticking their nasty old biographical prefaces up her ass.

Norman Mailer

"Burroughs may be gay, but he's a man..."

Burroughs may be gay, but he's a man. What I mean is that the fact that he's gay is incidental. He's very much a homosexual but when you meet him that's not what you think of him. You might think about him as a hermit, a mad prospector up in the mountains who'll shoot you if you come to his cabin at the wrong time. Or you can see him as a Vermont farmer who's been married to his wife for sixty years, and the day she dies someone says, "I guess you're going to miss her a lot, Zeke," and he says, "No, never did get to like her very much." So that he's got all those qualities, and on top of it all he is very much a homosexual, but that's somehow not the axis. He also has that way that certain people in society act, very formal, which is a defense against indiscreet inquiry, when let's say they've been put in jail for twenty years and they come out, and you can never refer to it in their presence, you wouldn't dream of it.

Gore Vidal

"We owed it to literary history..."

from PALIMPSEST

[On the night of August 23, 1953, Vidal and Kerouac, who knew each other slightly, met at the San Remo with Burroughs. From there, the three went on to Tony Pastor's, a lesbian bar. Kerouac drunkenly swung on a lamp-post afterward, "a Tarzan routine that caused Burroughs to leave us in disgust," Vidal recalled. Kerouac suggested that he and Vidal get a room somewhere, and with misgivings—Vidal preferred younger men, and Kerouac, at 31, was three years older—Vidal agreed. In *The Subterraneans*, Kerouac gave an otherwise factual, homo-censored account of the evening. Vidal supplied the missing details in a 1994 meeting with Allen Ginsberg, and in his memoir, *Palimpsest*.—ed.]

At the nearby Chelsea Hotel, each signed his real name. Grandly, I told the bemused clerk that this register would become famous. I've often wondered what did happen to it. Has anyone torn out our page? Or is it still hidden away in the dusty Chelsea files? Lust to one side, we both thought, even then (this was before *On the Road*), that we owed it to literary history to couple.

I remember that the bathroom was near the entrance to a large double room. There was no window shade, so a red neon light flickering on and off gave a rosy glow to the room and its contents. Jack was now in a manic mood: We must take a shower together. To my surprise, he was circumcised. Under the shower, for a moment, he rewound himself to the age of about fourteen and, for an instant, I saw not the dark slackly

---

muscled Jack but blond Jimmie,* only Jimmie was altogether more seri-ous and grown-up at fourteen than Jack...

I have just recalled Tennessee [Williams]'s aversion to sex with other writers or, indeed, with intellectuals of any kind. "It is most disturbing to think that the head beside you on the pillow might be thinking, too," said the Bird, who had a gift for selecting fine bodies attached to heads usually filled with the bright confetti of lunacy.

Where Anais [Nin] and I were incompatible—chicken hawk meets chicken hawk—Jack and I were an even more unlikely pairing—classic trade meets classic trade, and who will *do* what?

"Jack was rather proud of the fact that he blew you." Allen sounded a bit sad as we assembled our common memories over tea in the Hollywood Hills. I said that I had heard that Jack had announced the momentous feat to the entire clientele of the San Remo bar, to the con-sternation of one of the customers, an advertising man for Westinghouse, the firm that paid for the program *Studio One*, where I had only just begun to make a living as a television playwright. "I don't think," said the nervous advertiser, "that this is such a good advertisement for you, not to mention Westinghouse." As *On the Road* would not be published until 1957, he had no idea who Jack was.

Thanks to Allen's certainty of what Jack had told him, I finally recall the blow job—a pro forma affair, which I put a quick stop to. At what might be nicely called loose ends, we rubbed bellies for a while; later he would publish a poem dedicated to me: "Didn't know I was a great come-onner, did you? (come-on-er)." I was not particularly touched by this belated Valentine, considering that I finally flipped him over on his stomach, not an easy job as he was as much heavier than I as was the merchant mariner in Seattle,** whom he—only now does it strike me—physically resembled. Was I getting my own back on Jack's back?

---

* Jimmie Trimble, Vidal's boyhood love, who died in World War II.
** A memorable trick who had tried to flip the much-smaller but determinedly dominant Vidal onto his back.

—
36

Jack raised his head from the pillow to look at me over his left shoulder; off to our left the rosy neon from the window gave the room a mildly infernal glow. He stared at me for a moment—I see this part very clearly now, forehead half covered with sweaty dark curls—then he sighed as his head dropped back onto the pillow. There are other published versions of this encounter: In one, Jack says that he spent the night in the bathroom. On the floor? There was a shower but no tub. In another, he was impotent. But the potency of other males is, for me, a turn-off. What I have reported is all there was to it, except that I liked the way he smelled.

Gore Vidal

"Norman wanted to know what had really happened…"

from PALIMPSEST

For some reason Mailer and I drove back together to the city [from Vidal's country house] on that, or another, occasion. We were talking about Kerouac's *The Subterraneans*, and I said that I did not appreciate Jack's invasion of our common privacy. Norman wanted to know what had really happened. I told him. Norman almost drove us off the Taconic Parkway. Later, he worked up a mystical case that I had deliberately removed the steel from Jack's sphincter and that is why he took to drink and self-destruction.

Allen Ginsberg

"Something strange has happened..."

from a journal entry, January 8, 1961

Up walks several men, one I recognize & talk to—a middle-aged—perhaps Robert Lowell—but novelist—only later do I recognize Norman Mailer's on the same boat, first class, all along—He's wearing feminine bloomer clothers—a shirt that makes a lollypop round the hips & the breast—But his demeanor is the same manly one, only more schizamysterious and garbo-esque. Talking, after he leaves, with his companion, I suggest something strange has happened—They've already been to all ports in Mediterranean & are now returning back—have been to Algiers—I say I lived a while in Tanger—Mailer goes down to cabin, I follow. [...]

Going downstairs to Mess I sit next to Mailer who's brought his novelist's portfolio & is working on it—I decide to talk to him about his fantastic female dress and male body at the moment—he remains aloof & inviting & open.

Allen Ginsberg

"I sit naked in my room remembering..."

from a journal entry, June 17, 1951

Limping down the block, foot bruised yesterday in peyote euphoria on Washington Sq. with Keck & Anton.*

A boy came out of Shelley's, early twenties, in dungarees & striped T shirt—carrying 2 glasses of red liquor walking in front of me.

I sit naked in my room remembering the animal swing of his buttocks, the length and strength and paleness of his arms in the darkness as he balanced his way brushing slightly drunken against the granite of the building with his arm.

It is midnight in the blue attic,** summer, a thin film of sweat on my face.

He stopped after walking the length of the building down the side-street into the darkness, by an iron fence which led to an iron stairway down to a cement courtyard behind the building.

He put both glasses down, bending over—were they filled with wine—picked one up, and drank it all straight down. I walked on, staring back, he looked at me and said—

"I got a good deal out of the bar," or something.

"What a way to drink!" I said incoherently, walking on. I wanted to stop and make him—thinking of the crowd of youths around the pinball

* "Keck & Anton: members of a circle of seekers, some from West Coast, friends of Philip Lamantia & Carl Solomon, who hung around San Remo Bar MacDougal & Bleecker, Greenwich Village, at that time a center of Kerouac's N.Y. social life—described in *The Subterraneans*, late 40's & early 50's—A. G., September 1975" [note from *Journals: Early Fifties Early Sixties*].

** Ginsberg's New York apartment at that time, on 15th Street between 8th and 9th Avenues.

machine in the bar 2 months ago, the hunchback, the handsome one, the other boys—afraid of being discovered on the block as queer, or afraid of him & afraid to stop & talk. He was quite tall and evenly formed.

This reminds me—he not a great face [sic], just another momentary sadness of unobtainable common beauty—of the truly great strangers, the appearances of majesty I have seen on the streets here and there. A project which I have meant to sketch for several weeks.

In Houston, 1948—I was broke, stealing Pepsi Cola bottles to cash in and buy candy bars for hunger, waiting for a ship. Outside the old Union Hall, walking down the street, a Latin animal, Cuban, Spanish, I don't know. Electricity seemed to flow from his powerful body—black hair, curled wildly, looked impossible for him to live in society, to me—powerful malignant features—he was perhaps 22 or less—springing down the street in a tense potent walk, dungarees, powerful legs, not too tall, blue shirt opened several buttons on the chest, black hair curling sparsely on chest—he seemed made of iron, no sweat—or brown polished rock. I never in my life saw a more perfect being—expression of vigor and potency and natural rage on face—I couldn't conceive of him speaking English. I wondered what loves he had. Who could resist him? He must have taken any weak body he needed or wanted. Love from such a face I could not imagine, nor gentleness—but love and gentleness are not needed where there was so much life. He just passed me by and I stood there amazed staring at him as he disappeared up the block & around the corner scattering the air in spiritual waves behind him. I couldn't believe he was human. He had thick features, black eyebrows, almost square face, powerful chest, perfect freedom of walk.

Similar to him, the Latin I saw on 57th Street and Madison and Park, whom I followed down the street for several blocks, staring at him. This youth—he seemed very young, yet dressed impeccably in an Oxford grey or black suit, shining perfect black shoes, delicate grey tie—the clothes of a diplomat or rich artist—had long black hair combed neatly, like a statue or painting of perfect grooming, back on his head with a part—yet it was still a black animal mane. His features were regular and hard, very strong even face, with great force and dignity—all this in a youth not much older than me. I tagged along behind this culturally accomplished beast intelligence in my scuffed handmedown shoes, unpressed illfitting post adolescent suit, dirt ringed shirt and cheesy tie, hair askew and book underarm, perspiring perhaps. The impression of purpose & forcefulness, dignity, and social powerfulness embodied in this beautiful animal mask, the alien master man; a U.N. diplomat or courier I thought....

Finally a young kid in his middle teens perhaps walking with a few boys down Market Street, Paterson, past City hall, past the bank and Schoonmakers [a Paterson, New Jersey, department store], 3 years ago or 2, when I was wandering downtown around, don't remember why. He had neither the bestial brilliance of the Spaniard, nor suffering nor intellectuality of others, nor their age: he was rather short, and at first glance perhaps even too short (stunted by cigarettes?), dressed in dungarees, very tight: he was well built though, thick buttocks and short powerful genitals pressing out the tight workpants, and perhaps a dirty t-shirt over the wide squat chest (he was not however a dwarf, just a small powerful adolescent)—and a plain, not ugly, not nice face—yet as I first glanced at him and passed by I felt almost faint from the wave of dirty sexuality, of real knowing naive, innocent carnality; physical liberty, belly and buttock power in him. He walked down the street and I half followed I was so struck—my own body reacted to his like a magnet to a magnet disturbed and drawn, sickened in the belly by lust—the frankness of his body—he was talking to several other gangling unformed adolescents, he smoked a cigarette freely, talking perhaps describing some conquest, perhaps occupied in some showy-manly plot for a secret club or hide-out. I never saw anyone I wanted to lock my body with so strongly—except perhaps the savage Spaniard of Houston.

Diane di Prima

"It was a strange, nondescript kind of orgy..."

[Diane di Prima was part of the East Village poetry scene from the early 1950s. Very much a bohemian, she read and wrote constantly, sacrificing physical comfort for the luxury of words. She also had many lovers, including the poet LeRoi Jones, then married to Hettie Jones and, like di Prima, mildly bisexual at that time. Together, they edited the Beat-associated mimeographed newsletter *The Floating Bear* and helped carry on the battle against censorship. *Memoirs of a Beatnik* was a written-for-hire erotic autobiography, and is rich with incidental details of hipster life.—ed.]

I had been in sporadic correspondence with Allen Ginsberg and some of his friends ever since I read *Howl* (Lawrence Ferlinghetti had even written a tiny introduction for my "unpublishable" first book).* Now Allen and his gang were in New York and I was eager to meet them. After a few phone calls back and forth they came down to Leslie's,** where I was staying, bringing with them a great quantity of cheap wine and some very good grass. We all proceeded to get thoroughly stoned, and Allen and Jack Kerouac, who was with him, rapped down a long, beautiful high-flown rap all about poetry and high endeavor. Jack's belief, which Allen shared at the time, was that one should never change or rewrite anything. He felt that the initial flash of the turned-on mind was best, in life as well as in poetry, and I could see that he probably really lived that

---

* *This Bird Flies Backward* (1958). Friends had advised her that no one would publish the book because the black street slang she used was incomprehensible to readers.
** Leslie (no last name given), a dancer friend of di Prima's. His lover of the moment was a man named Benny Hudson, who "smelled of soap and earnestness and other Midwestern values" (di Prima, *Memoirs of a Beatnik*, 179).

—

way. He seized upon my notebooks and proceeded to uncorrect the poems, rolling the original bumpy lines off his tongue, making the stops and awkwardnesses beautiful while we all got higher and higher.

I proposed that they spend the night. Allen had eyes for Leslie and agreed readily, enlisting his lover Peter's help in moving the couch from the front room to the back, and setting it beside the double bed. They were about the same height and made one extra-wide, only slightly bumpy, sleeping place. They dragged the whole thing into the center of the room, arranged plants around it, and burning sticks of Indian incense which they stuck into the flower pots. Benny watched, horrified.

After kissing us all lingeringly, Peter split—to what mysterious night rituals of his own, we could only surmise. Leslie lit some candles and placed them at the bedside, turning off the overhead light. Immediately, the room seemed immense, mysterious, the beds an island, a camp in a great forest wilderness (Leslie's rubber plants). We all undressed—Benny with some trepidation—and climbed on.

It was a strange, nondescript kind of orgy. Allen set things going by largely and fully embracing all of us, each in turn and all at once, sliding from body to body in a great wallow of flesh. It was warm and friendly and very unsexy—like being in a bathtub with four other people. To make matters worse, I had my period, and was acutely aware of the little white string of a tampax sticking out of my cunt. I played for a while with the cocks with which I found myself surrounded, planning as soon as I could to get out of the way of the action and go to sleep.

But Jack was straight, and finding himself in a bed with three faggots and me, he wanted some pussy and decided he was going to get it. He began to persuade me to remove the tampax by nuzzling and nudging at my breasts and neck with his handsome head. Meanwhile everyone else was urging me to join in the games. Allen embarked on a long speech on the joys of making it while menstruating: the extra lubrication, the extra excitement due to a change of hormones, animals in heat bleed

—

slightly, etc. Finally, to the cheer of the whole gang, I pulled out the bloody talisman and flung it across the room.

Having done his part to assure a pleasurable evening for Jack and myself, Allen fell to work on the young male bodies beside him, and was soon wrapped round, with Leslie on one side of him and Benny on the other. I heard some squeals, and felt much humping and bumping about, but in the welter of bedclothes the action was rather obscure. Jack began by gallantly going down on me to prove that he didn't mind a little blood. He had a wildly nestling, hugging sort of approach, and he was a big man; I was taken over, and lay there with legs spead and eyes closed while he snorted and leaped like Pan. When I shut my eyes I was once more aware of the warm ocean of flesh around me, could distinguish the various love-sounds and breathings of all other creatures.

We finally got loose of the bedclothes: Jack, with a great cry, heaved himself upwards and dumped them all on the floor, then fell heavily on top of me and entered me immediately. My momentary surprise turned to pleasure, and I squirmed down on his cock, getting it all inside of me, feeling good and full. It nudged the neck of my womb, and I felt a thrill of a different kind, a pleasure that, starting in my groin, spread outward to the edge of my skin, stirring every hair follicle on my body separately. We bucked and shifted, looking for the best position, fucked for a long time on our sides. Then Jack withdrew and flipped over on his back. I played with his half-soft cock with the traces of my blood on it, bringing it back to fullness. He indicated by gestures that he wanted me to sit on top of him. I did, guiding his cock inside me, and it touched the same place at the neck of my womb again, but this time more heavily, so that the pleasure was sharper and edged with a slight pain.

It was a long, slow, easy fuck. I knelt with my feet tucked under me and moved up and down on Jack's cock while his hands on my waist supported and guided my movement. I glanced at the group beside me. Leslie was lying on Allen, kissing him, and they were grinding their stomachs together. I could imagine, though I could not see, their two

—

hard cocks between then, denting the soft skin of their bellies. Benny lay a little to one side of the two of them. He was kissing Leslie's back and neck, and he had his own cock in his hand. Pleasure began to increase in my gut, I bent down and kissed Jack on the mouth, moving faster and faster against him. His two hands on my shoulders held me warm and tight, as we both came in the friendliness of that huge, candlelit room.

Jack stirred after a few minutes of light rest. He leaned over the side of the bed, feeling around to find his soft leather pouch, and rolled a joint of good Mexican grass. Drew on it deeply and handed it to me. I smoked a little, and looked around to see where the others were at. Allen was lying full out on the bed, and Leslie was fucking him in the ass. I tried to hand the joint to Benny, who refused it with a shake of his head and fell, sobbing, into my arms. I handed the grass back to Jack, and tried to comfort Benny, but he would only lie there, sobbing softly. I stroked his shoulders and back and wished he would stop. It was very boring. Jack caught my eye and grinned at my chagrin. I turned my head towards him and he put the grass back in my mouth, holding it for me while I drew on it. Finally Benny stopped and said, "I have to go to the bathroom." He tromped about with reproachful noises, finding a bathrobe, and was lost in the unfathomed halls and staircases.

Allen and Leslie finished doing their thing, and Leslie was hungry, as he always was after fucking, and went to the kitchen and came back with bread and herring and a bag of early peaches, and he and Jack and I sat munching and smoking, while Allen scribbled in a notebook, occasionally looking up abstractedly for the grass. Jack pulled me between his legs and began to rub his limp cock against my backside and eventually got it hard again, and he exclaimed, "Look, Allen!" and leaped out of bed pulling me onto him as he stood in a deep plié and we tried to do it in Tibetan yab-yum position. It felt good, was really fine lots of fun, but Jack was drunk and high and balance not too good, and we fell over, narrowly missing a plant, and went on fucking on the floor, my legs around his waist, while he protested that we should slow down and let him get into lotus position so we could try that one. But I simply locked my ankles around his waist, spread the cheeks of his ass with my hands, kept him busy, and we flipped over first one way and then the other on the floor.

Allen by this time was reciting Whitman and rubbing Leslie's cock with his feet...

II.

Male Muses

(Or, Sex without Borders)

Without Neal Cassady, there would be no *On the Road*, no *Visions of Cody*, and none of the powerful poems Ginsberg would write for him, like "The Green Automobile" or "On Neal's Ashes." Without Kerouac, there would be no *Howl*. Without Ginsberg, there would be no *Naked Lunch*. Just as important as the Beats' mutual attraction and influence was the fact that their romantic desires for each other were usually thwarted or triangulated. Ginsberg loved Carr and Kerouac, and then Cassady. Cassady loved Ginsberg, but not in the same way. Burroughs loved Ginsberg, who loved him back, but not as much. Had there been direct, requited, unhampered love between any two Beats, they would have paired off and broken the circle. Longing is a better muse than satisfaction. It was not in the first flush of love, for example, but during a troubled separation from his new lover, Peter Orlovsky, that Ginsberg entered the state of mind in which he began *Howl*. This is true, as well, of the routines Burroughs spun in his letters to Ginsberg from Tangier, many of which would end up in *Naked Lunch*. They are a lover's appeal—a courtship display, like the fanning of plumage. Although they had their genesis in the four months in 1953 that he and Ginsberg had lived together in New York, they might never have surfaced if Ginsberg hadn't finally rejected him, blurting out "But I don't want your ugly old cock!"*

---

* Ginsberg had ferocious verbal reflexes when tapped in the right spot. In their Columbia days, Kerouac called him "Jewboy" until Ginsberg snapped, "You eat shit from your mother's cunt!"

Taking this hint, Burroughs left alone for Tangier and began to write the letters that a contrite Ginsberg would praise and preserve and eventually help edit into *Naked Lunch*. It was Kerouac and Ginsberg who had convinced Burroughs to write in the first place, and both would later type his manuscript—that womanly act of devotion—though Kerouac had to quit when it gave him nightmares. The intensity of desire that had frightened away Ginsberg—the need to "schlup," to merge like jellied blobs of protoplasm—was still potent on the page. Kerouac's free-flowing, jazz-inspired *Dr. Sax* is a tribute of sorts to Burroughs and is saturated with the voice readers would later come to know in *Naked Lunch*. (In a typical collaborative flourish, Ginsberg gave Kerouac the novel's Shakespearean ending.) Although productive on their own, the three were entirely tied up in each other's writing lives throughout the 1950s. *Howl* may have been dedicated to Ginsberg's friend Carl Solomon, but was in fact the fruit of Kerouac's influence on Ginsberg. And Ginsberg served as agent for both Burroughs and Kerouac, taking on a world of trouble. His biographer, Barry Miles, argues that Ginsberg "single-handedly willed the Beat Generation into being by his unshakeable belief that his poet friends were all geniuses."*

As a muse, it is hard to beat Neal Cassady, who added tremendous native intelligence and curiosity to the requisite youth and good looks. Bigger-than-life, though ultimately unreachable, he strung along both Kerouac and Ginsberg for years, drawing them out west to Denver, San Francisco, San Jose, promising a heady blend of adventure, male bonding, and admiration for their writing.** His ambition was to write, though his gift was for speech. In one of his rambling, inspired, single-spaced, typed letters to Ginsberg, he admitted that in his earliest efforts he would change words—even meanings—rather than correct a typing error, and would gamely follow the new word wherever it led. He knew

* Miles, 212.
** He made rakish use of one of Allen's love poems to him in March 1947, when he read it aloud to Carolyn Robinson, his future wife. She only later learned that Neal had not written the poem for her.

his life would make fantastic copy, if only he could stop twitching long enough to write. For Ginsberg, he was a classic object of desire—the lean, hard alpha male of his sex poem, "Please, Master," written months after Cassady's death in 1968:

> ...please master order me down on the floor,
> please master tell me to lick your thick shaft
> please master put your rough hands on my bald hairy skull
> please master press my mouth to your prick-heart

Yet it was Kerouac, the disciplined writer and notebook-keeper, who would capture the hyperkinetic Cassady on paper, absorbing his mannerisms, inhabiting his mind, serving up his stories in a brilliantly mimicked voice.

Throughout the winter and spring of 1951, Cassady wrote hard. He worked on his memoirs, and churned out twenty- and thirty-page letters to his friends. The famous "Joan Anderson" letter emerged in these fertile months: the 23,000-word confession to Kerouac about an early girlfriend who had had an abortion for Cassady, then waited for him to pick her up while he and a friend got drunk in a nearby bar. Recognizing the power of what he'd written, Cassady explained that his method was to push ahead without stopping or questioning himself. He didn't change a word. He wrote straight through on a Benzedrine high. Stunned by the power and fluency of the letter, Kerouac told anyone who would listen: "Neal is a colossus risen to Destroy Denver!" In April, stricken with what Ginsberg later described as "puppy love," Kerouac sat down at the typewriter in his Manhattan apartment, inserted one end of a roll of Chinese paper, and hammered out *On the Road* in twenty days. It worked like voodoo. By mid-May, Cassady was complaining to Ginsberg that he hadn't written in a month: "There is a dissatisfaction; a basic deeply disgusting impatience and feeling of overwhelming inadequacy with words." Soon his letters dried up, too. As Kerouac took possession of his voice, gestures, and childhood memories, Cassady weakened. Even if he had managed to write more than the autobiographical fragments of *The First Third* (posthumously published in 1971), he would have had little fresh material.

In a 1965 *Paris Review* interview, Ginsberg described William Burroughs as "a very *tender* sort of person, but very dignified and shy and withdrawn." He was also the only one in the circle who seemed immune to Cassady's charms.* What Burroughs liked in a young man was a capacity for intimacy. He did not need to be entertained. On the contrary, he needed a receptive audience—a "receiver"—for his routines. "I don't see myself writing any sequel to *Queer* or writing anything more at all at this point. I wrote *Queer* for Marker," he told Ginsberg in October 1952. "I guess he doesn't think much of it or me." The owlish, barely bisexual Lewis Marker, Burroughs's boyfriend in Mexico, had read the novel and told him, "Well, it's not a bad yarn, but don't get the idea you're anything in the way of a writer."** Burroughs's feelings of hopelessness eddied out from his writing to his chances at love: "I don't see myself going through this deal again, and of course the possibility of mutual attraction is remote."***

The admiring Ginsberg made a far more satisfying receiver, especially considering that Kerouac, in an attempt to comfort Burroughs, had suggested that Ginsberg wanted him after all. Yet Ginsberg, who was traveling, did not always get Burroughs's letters, or post quick responses. Lonely and panicked, Burroughs wrote Cassady and Kerouac from Tangier, begging for news of Ginsberg, and then confessed, in an April

---

* Nevertheless, "course Bull [Bill] and I slept together one night, too," said Cassady on the tapes transcribed by Kerouac in *Visions of Cody*.
** Morgan, 214.
*** Harris, 138. Later, sympathizing with Ginsberg over Cassady's withdrawal, Burroughs suggested that he lower his sights. Couldn't he find someone like Burroughs's Tangier boyfriend Kiki: "sweet and affectionate, but indubitably masculine? Of course [such a companion] is never going to fall madly in love with *you*. That's obvious."

1954 letter: "Dear Allen, I have written and rewritten this for you. So please answer."

> Routines like habit. Without routines my life is chronic night-mare, gray horror of midwest suburb....
>
> I have to have receiver for routine. If there is no one there to receive it, routine turns back on me like homeless curse and tears me apart, grows more and more insane (literal growth like cancer) and impossible, and fragmentary like berserk pin-ball machine and I am screaming, "Stop it! Stop it!"*

The calm, complete acceptance and deep union that Burroughs had been looking for with Ginsberg during those months in New York, Ginsberg was soon to find in San Francisco with a pretty young man named Peter Orlovsky. They met around Christmas of 1954, in the apartment of the painter Robert LaVigne, then Orlovsky's boyfriend. In an interview in *Gay Sunshine* almost twenty years later, Ginsberg described the raptures of his first night with Orlovsky, of "completely giving and taking." "With Jack or Neal," he explained, "with people who were primarily heterosexual and who didn't fully accept the sexualization of tenderness, I felt I was forcing it on them; so I was always very timid about them making love back to me, and they very rarely did very much. When they did, it was like blessings from heaven."** Orlovsky, too, was primarily heterosexual, but this didn't seem an obstacle at the beginning. Sweet-natured and vulnerable, he made a vow with Ginsberg that they would own each other, body and soul: "Total interpossession was what we decided. It was a very strange, illuminating subjective moment, with the burden of fear and doubt falling off for

* Harris, 201.
** Cassady/Ginsberg, March 30, 1947: "I really don't know how much I can be satisfied to love you, I mean bodily, you know I, somehow, dislike pricks & men & before you, had consciously forced myself to be homosexual," i.e. to hustle. Cassady explained that he'd been forcing physical desire for Ginsberg to compensate for all he was learning from him.

both of us."* Ginsberg had the intellect, it was agreed, and Orlovsky the beauty. It seemed a perfect exchange.

There was the little matter of Ginsberg's girlfriend, Sheila Boucher, however, who got "cold and annoyed" when Ginsberg told her about Cassady and Orlovsky. "It was as if my thing with men had really bugged her, put her off," Ginsberg recalled. "I was like saying, Why don't we *all* go to bed together, but for some reason she got mad at that."**

There was no problem, it seemed, that group sex could not resolve. When Ginsberg brought Orlovsky with him to Tangier to visit Burroughs the next year, they decided to override the older writer's jealousy by exhausting him sexually. "We went to Tangier to fuck Bill," as Ginsberg put it. It worked at first, and the three got along reasonably well while Ginsberg helped pull the stained, repetitive, disordered pages of *Naked Lunch* into publishable form. But Burroughs was not charmed by Orlovsky, who freely approached Moroccans on the streets of Tangier and could not be convinced of his bad manners. Mental illness ran in Orlovsky's family, and the army had discharged him as a psych case. He was a free spirit, but also, clearly, a nut. (He told Ginsberg's biographer, Jane Kramer, that his *sadhana* was cleaning. He carried rags, and would wipe down surfaces wherever he went. His one volume of verse was titled *Clean Asshole Poems and Smiling Vegetable Songs*.) When Burroughs's friend Alan Ansen came from Venice to help with the editing, he told Burroughs that Orlovsky was "a freeloading bitch posing as an assistant mahatma."*** The strained trio fell apart over Burroughs's feelings about women, which stung Orlovsky so much that he left. Relations failed to improve over the coming years, when queer friends Ian Sommerville and Brion Gysin (later, in London, the groupie Michael Portman) brought out all of Burroughs's latent misogyny. "I think they [women] were a basic mistake," Burroughs would write later, in *The Job* (1968),

* Kramer, 45.
** Ibid.
*** Morgan, 266.

"and the whole dualistic universe evolved from this error. Women are no longer necessary for reproduction."

Burroughs's basic discomfort with women was not dispelled by a heterosexual crisis in the late 1950s, which coincided with the loss of his boyfriend Kiki and his attempts to kick drugs. "I find my eyes straying towards the fair sex," he confessed to Ginsberg:

(It's the new *frisson*, dearie... Women are downright piquant.) You hear about these old characters find out they are queer at fifty, maybe I'm about to make with the switcheroo. What are these strange feelings that come over me when I look at a young cunt's little tits sticking out so cute? Could it be that?? No! No! He thrust the thought from him in horror. He stumbled out into the street with the girl's mocking laughter lingering in his ears, laughter that seemed to say, "Who you think you're kidding with the queer act? I know you, baby."*

These feelings arose for Burroughs in part because of the psychic struggle of his work on *Naked Lunch*. He was wrestling with his identity, and sometimes losing. But he was also lonely and disgusted with himself for wanting what he could not find: a masculine companion who could hold his interest. In moments like these, he could write that queerness was a horrible sickness—at least for him—and that he was about to cancel his "sado-masochistic visa to Sodom." "Must have some cunt," he exclaimed, "I was never supposed to be queer at all. The whole original trauma is out now."** The panic began to subside, however, when he left Tangier for the "Beat Hotel" in Paris in 1958 and formed a creative partnership with the artist and writer Brion Gysin: more a collaborator than a muse, more a friend than a receiver.

* Burroughs/Ginsberg, Sept. 16, 1956, Harris, 326–27.
** Burroughs/Ginsberg, Nov. 26, 1957, Harris, 378.

—

Jack Kerouac

"Oh, I love, love, love women!"

from ON THE ROAD

We were suddenly driving along the blue waters of the Gulf, and at the same time a momentous mad thing began on the radio; it was the Chicken Jazz'n Gumbo disk-jockey show from New Orleans, all mad jazz records, colored records, with the disk jockey saying, "Don't worry 'bout *nothing!*" We saw New Orleans in the night ahead of us with joy. Dean rubbed his hands over the wheel. "Now we're going to get our kicks!" At dusk we were coming into the humming streets of New Orleans. "Oh, smell the people!" yelled Dean with his face out the window, sniffing. "Ah! God! Life!" He swung around a trolley. "Yes!" He darted the car and looked in every direction for girls. "Look at *her!*" The air was so sweet in New Orleans it seemed to come in soft bandannas; and you could smell the river and really smell the people, and mud, and molasses, and every kind of tropical exhalation with your nose suddenly removed from the dry ices of a Northern winter. We bounced in our seats. "And dig her!" yelled Dean, pointing at another woman. "Oh, I love, love, love women!"* He spat out the window; he groaned; he clutched his head. Great beads of sweat fell from his forehead from pure excitement and exhaustion.

* Dean Moriarty is the Neal Cassady character in *On the Road*. The narrator is Sal Paradise, based on Kerouac. It's worth noting that Moriarty's new wife "Marylou" (LuAnne Henderson in life) is sitting beside him during his raptures on the fair sex.

—

Neal Cassady

"I'm on a spree tonight..."

from a letter to Allen Ginsberg, April 10, 1947

[After escaping his affair with Ginsberg by fleeing back to Denver, Cassady sent several letters alternately rejecting Ginsberg and cajoling him into joining Cassady in the West, though on terms that could not possibly benefit Ginsberg. Ginsberg wrote back, calling Cassady a "dirty, double-crossing, faithless bitch." But he did, in the end, allow himself to be lured across the country—more than once—for further episodes of frustration and humiliation.—ed.]

I'm on a spree tonight, I'll tell you exactly what *I* want, giving no thought to you, or any respect or consideration to your feelings.

First, I want to stay here and drive a cab until July, second, go to Texas and see Bill and Joan for a few weeks, third, (perhaps) dig New Orleans with Jack, fourth, be in N.Y. by early Sept, find an apt., go to college (as much as they'll let me) work on a parking lot again, and live with a girl *and* you. Fifth, leave N. Y. in June '48 and go to Europe for the summer.

I don't care what you think, that's what I want. If you are able to understand and can see your way clear to sheparding me around the big city for 9 months, then, perhaps, go to Europe with me next summer that's swell, great and wonderful, exactly what I want, if not—well, why not? really, damn it, why not? You sense I'm not worthy of you? you think I wouldn't fit it? you presume I'd treat you as badly or worse? You feel I'm not bright enough? you know I'd be imposing, or demanding, or trying to suck you dry of all you have intellectually? Or is it just that you

—

are, almost unconsciously, aware of enough lack of interest in me, or indifference to my plight and need of you, to believe that all the trouble of helping and living with me, would not be quite compensated for by being with me? I can't promise a damn thing, I know I'm bisexual, but prefer women, there's a slimmer line than you think between my attitude toward love and yours, don't be so concerned, it'll fall into line. Beyond that—who knows? Let's try it and see, huh?

I like your latest poems, in fact, I like most of your poems, through reading more poetry I've become a bit better able to judge and appreciate your work.

Relax, man, think about what I say and try to see yourself moving toward me without any compulsive demands, due to lack of assurance that I love you, or because of lack of belief that I understand you etc. forget all that and in that forgetfulness see if there isn't more peace of mind and even more physical satisfaction than in your present subjective longing (whether for me, or Lucien, or anybody) I know one cannot alter by this method, but come to me with all you've got, throw your demands in my face, (for I love them) and find a true closeness, not only because what emotionally I have is also distorted by lonliness, but also because I, logically or not, feel I want you more than anyone at this stage.

I'm really beat, off to bed, and a knowledge of relief, for I *know* that you must understand and move with me in this, you better not fight against it or any other damn thing, so shut up, relax, find some patience and fit into my mellow plans.

Love + Kisses, my boy, opps!, excuse, I'm not Santa Claus am I?
Well then, just—Love + Kisses,
Neal

Allen Ginsberg

"Love is not controllable..."

from a letter to Carolyn Cassady, June [?] 1952

[From January to May 1952, while hiding from his wife, Joan, and her court orders for child support, Jack Kerouac lived with Neal Cassady and his family at 29 Russell Street in San Francisco. It was a rocky visit, at first, with Carolyn feeling like a household drudge, and Jack and Neal constrained to stay home and sober at least part of the time. Soon, Neal encouraged a love affair between his wife and his old friend, and, on one of Neal's trips out of town, they complied. Thereafter, she was much happier with her houseguest— "I served whichever was in residence, according to their individual requirements," she recounts in her memoir, *Heart Beat*—and also rose in the esteem of Allen Ginsberg. When Jack left, and failed to write to Neal or Carolyn for a month, and Neal reverted to depression and inattentiveness, she wrote to Allen for advice. Relishing the role, he responded in detail.—ed.]

Jack's attitude:

a) As I haven't got all his letters here, I'll send on an anthology of statements apropos his relations with Neal when I assemble them. What *I* think about it is, Jack loves Neal platonically (which I think is a pity, but maybe about sex I'm "projecting," as the analysts say), and Neal loves Jack, too. The fact is that Jack is very inhibited, however. However, also sex doesn't define the whole thing.

b) Jack still loves Neal no less than ever.

c) Jack ran into a blank wall which everyone understands and respects in Neal, including Jack and Neal. It upset and dispirited Jack, made

—

him feel lonely and rejected and like a little brother whose questions the older brother wouldn't answer.

d) Jack loves Carolyn also, though obviously not with the same intensity and power as he loves Neal, and this is acceptable and obvious considering all the parties involved, their history together, how much they knew each other and how often they lived thru the same years and crises. Jack is full of Carolyn's praises and nominates her to replace Joan Burroughs as Ideal Mother image, Madwoman, chick and ignu. The last word means a special honorary type post-hip intellectual. Its main root is ignoramus from the mythology of W. C. Fields. Jack also says Carolyn beats Dusty* for mind.

e) Jack said nothing about sleeping with you in his letters.

f) Jack thinks Neal is indifferent to him, however only in a special way, as he realizes how good Neal has been to him and that Neal really loves him; but they couldn't communicate I guess. However, he would love to live all together with everybody in Mexico, I believe. He would claim right to treat Neal as a human being and hit him on the breast with balloons. I will transmit all messages immediately.

g) I did not think (even dream) from Neal's note he is bitter. I was surprised to get his invitation to visit, and thought it showed great gentility in the writing and the proposal which I accept with rocky belly for sometime in the future. Had I money I would fly out immediately for weekends by plane.

h) Perhaps Neal wants to feel like a crestfallen cuckold because he wants to be beat on the breast with balloons. I well imagine him in that position. Neal's last confession is perhaps yet to be made, tho his salvation is already assured...however nobody seems to take seriously the confessions he has made already and continues to do so, which have alwasy had ring of innocency and childlike completeness and have been all he knows, which is more (about himself) than anybody else knows anyway. I believe Neal.

* Dusty Moreland, an artist girlfriend of Ginsberg's during a promiscuously hetero period of his life.

—

I include his preoccupation and blankness (preoccupation with R. R., household moneying, etc., as final confessions of great merit and value, representing truth to him.

What further sweetness and juiciness issues therefrom no one knows, even him; there is no forcing anything, guilt. (He does not know?) He is already on top of the world. What to do with world is next problem.

Jack probably feels no remorse, just compassion for Neal.

I don't know whether you do or don't want to make Neal feel jealous… it's a question for you to answer, but perhaps it is not important to answer it, or it can't be ultimately.

Jack's Mexican plans may or may not go through. Mexico may be a good idea for all of us when we become properly solidified.

Love is not controllable; it can only be offered and accepted…you know…under the right conditions. As a matter of general course I accept your love and return my own, but it will take a moment of soul-facing and intensity to actually communicate other than words and hopes and general feelings. I don't *know* you like I know Neal, and love is only knowledge. Don't get me wrong. This is no rejection of your desire to come in the middle of the hazy circle, which itself knoweth itself not. Let us arrange all elements to be physically present then.

I am not shipping out I am sure after all.

The moment is ripe for me to be in S.F. South America with Bill and maybe Jack and in N.Y., and I can't be in all three at once. I wish we were all together however. How have we become so scattered?

What we must make plans to do is all meet somewhere where it is practically possible for us to live, under our various pressures, when the practical time comes. Shall we not then keep it in mind to try to arrange for a total grand reunion somewhere for as long as it can last?

I am definitely interested in going to bed with everybody and making love…however also I want to say my sexual life has changed a little and with Neal I want him to make love to me. This is something know, as if the jigsaw puzzle were falling into place. He understands that.

—

The mileage is too great; we are being tossed around in the cosmic mixing machines. I will make what arrangements I can think of.

Love, Allen

P.S. Neal: Write me a letter about sex.

A.

William Burroughs

Bradley the Buyer

from NAKED LUNCH

[Burroughs's famous "Bradley the Buyer" routine is a nightmare vision of homosexual longing that manages to incorporate several of its author's recurrent themes: control, addiction, physical rot, and the bureaucratic menace.—ed.]

Mexico City where Lupita sits like an Aztec Earth Goddess doling out her little papers of lousy shit.

"Selling is more of a habit than using," Lupita says. Nonusing pushers have a contact habit, and that's one you can't kick. Agents get it too. Take Bradley the Buyer. Best narcotics agent in the industry. Anyone would make him for junk. (Note: Make in the sense of dig or size up.) I mean he can walk up to a pusher and score direct. He is so anonymous, grey and spectral the pusher don't remember him afterwards. So he twists one after the other....

Well the buyer comes to look more and more like a junky. He can't drink. He can't get it up. His teeth fall out. (Like pregnant women lose their teeth feeding the stranger, junkies lose their yellow fangs feeding the monkey.) He is all the time sucking on a candy bar. Baby Ruths he digs special. "It really disgust you to see the Buyer sucking on them candy bars so nasty," a cop says.

The Buyer takes on an ominous grey-green color. Fact is his body is making its own junk or the equivalent. The Buyer has a steady connection. A Man Within you might say. Or so he thinks. "I'll just set in my room," he says. "Fuck 'em all. Squares on both sides. I am the only complete man in the industry."

But a yen comes on him like a great black wind through the bones. So the buyer hunts up a young junky and gives him a paper to make it.

"Oh all right," the boys says. "So what you want to make?"

"I just want to rub up against you and get fixed."

"Ugh... Well all right.... But why cancha just get physical like a human?"

Later the boy is sitting in a Waldorf with two colleagues dunking pound cake. "Most distasteful thing I ever stand still for," he says. "Some way he make himself all soft like a blob of jelly and surround me so nasty. Then he gets wet all over like with green slime. So I guess he come to some kinda awful climax.... I come near wigging with that green stuff all over me, and he stink like an old rotten cantaloupe."

"Well it's still an easy score."

The boy sighed resignedly; "Yes, I guess you can get used to anything. I've got a meet with him again tomorrow."

The Buyer's habit keeps getting heavier. He needs a recharge every half hour. Sometimes he cruises the precincts and bribes the turnkey to let him in with a cell of junkies. It get to where no amount of contact will fix him. At this point he receives a summons from the District Supervisor:

"Bradley, your conduct has given rise to rumors—and I hope for your sake they are no more than that—so unspeakably distasteful that... I mean Caesar's wife...hrump...that is, the Department must be above suspicion...certainly above such suspicions as you have seemingly aroused. You are lowering the entire tone of the industry. We are prepared to accept your immediate resignation."

The Buyer throws himself on the ground and crawls over to the D. S. "No, Boss Man, no... The Department is my very lifeline."

He kisses the D. S.'s hand thrusting his fingers into his mouth (the D. S. must feel his toothless gums) complaining he has lost his teeth "inna thervith." "Please Boss Man. I'll wipe your ass, I'll wash out your dirty condoms, I'll polish your shoes with the oil on my nose...."

"Really, this is most distasteful! Have you no pride? I must tell you I feel a distinct revulsion. I mean there is something, well, rotten about you, and you smell like a compost heap." He put a scented handkerchief in front of his face. "I must ask you to leave this office at once."

"I'll do anything, Boss, anything." His ravaged green face splits into a horrible smile. "I'm still young, Boss, and I'm pretty strong when I get my blood up."

The D. S. retches into his handkerchief and points to the door with a limp hand. The Buyer stands up looking at the D. S. dreamily. His body begins to dip like a dowser's wand. He flows forward....

"No! No!" screams the D. S.

"Schlup...schlup schlup." An hour later they find the Buyer on the nod in the D. S.'s chair. The D. S. has disappeared without a trace.

The Judge: "Everything indicates that you have, in some unspeakable manner uh...assimilated the District Supervisor. Unfortunately there is no proof. I would recommend that you be confined or more accurately contained in some institution, but I know of no place suitable for a man of your caliber. I must reluctantly order your release."

"That one should stand in an aquarium," says the arresting officer.

The Buyer spreads terror throughout the industry. Junkies and agents disappear. Like a vampire bat he gives off a narcotic effluvium, a dank green mist that anesthetizes his victims and renders them helpless in his enveloping presence. And once he has scored he holes up for several days like a gorged boa constrictor. Finally he is caught in the act of digesting the Narcotics Commissioner and destroyed with a flame thrower—the court of inquiry ruling that such means were justified in that the Buyer had lost his human citizenship and was, in consequence, a creature without species and a menace to the narcotics industry on all levels.

Jack Kerouac

"Posterity will laugh at me..."

from a letter to Neal Cassady, October 3, 1948

I consider queerness a hostility, not a love. "Woman exists because there was man—the penis exists because first there was void—(cunt)—therefore, "I have one of my own" (a void, or a penis)—"You have one of your own—you do not *really* wish mine without envy, hostility, aggression, and inverted desire." These are my views.... (SILLY) (SELF CONSCIOUS TOO)...and I'm not saying them for *your* benefit (don't have to) so much as for "posterity" which may someday read this letter, all my letters (as Kerouac).* Posterity will laugh at me if it thinks I was queer... little students will be disillusioned. By that time science & feelings intuitive will have shown it is VICE, VICIOUS, not love, gentle...and Kerouac will be a goat, pitied. I fight that. I am *not* a fool! a queer! I am *not!* He-he! Understand? And forgive me for dramatizing the idiotic thoughts I have at moments. They're of no use to you. I am the Sly Idiot, I refuse to be accused of concealing anything. I am sad, and mad, and I wish I could be sensible like you & Paul & my sister & my mother & Ann etc.

Jack

P.S. Neal, all your doubts about the semi-fertilized intelligence of my mind must be confirmed by this letter. Are they? And what would others say? Neal, pretty soon I'm going to start saying & doing what I please and cease trying to be a "model" truth-speaker for mankind. The prophet is always false to himself, therefore hates himself. Right? Tell me.

* Kerouac's concern for posterity is curious, since he was at this time an unknown writer, whose first novel, *The Town and the City*, would not be published until March 1950.

—

Allen Ginsberg

Love Poem on Theme by Whitman

I'll go into the bedroom silently and lie down between the bridegroom
    and the bride,
those bodies fallen from heaven stretched out waiting naked and restless,
arms resting over their eyes in the darkness,
bury my face in their shoulders and breasts, breathing their skin,
and stroke and kiss neck and mouth and make back be open and known,
legs raised up crook'd to receive, cock in the darkness driven tormented
    and attacking
roused up from hole to itching head,
bodies locked shuddering naked, hot hips and buttocks screwed into
    each other
and eyes, eyes glinting and charming, widening into looks and
    abandon,
and moans of movement, voices, hands in air, hands between thighs,
hands in moisture on softened lips, throbbing contraction of bellies
till the white come flow in the swirling sheets,
and the bride cry for forgiveness, and the groom be covered with tears of
    passion and compassion,
and I rise up from the bed replenished with last intimate gestures and
    kisses of farewell—
all before the mind wakes, behind shades and closed doors in a
    darkened house
where the inhabitants roam unsatisfied in the night,
nude ghosts seeking each other out in the silence.

1954

—
77

Elise Cowen

Teacher—Your Body My Kabbalah

[A haunting presence in the Beat afterlife, Elise Cowen was a brilliant, quirky Barnard College student whose unconventional friends and manners earned her the campus nickname "Beat Alice." She told her friend Leo Skir that she stole from libraries and bookstores because it was "the only moral way to get books." Cowen was Ginsberg's girlfriend through the spring and summer of 1953. Later, she and a female lover lived with Allen and Peter. Her close friend, the poet and novelist Joyce Johnson, has written: "Elise was a moment in Allen's life. In Elise's life, Allen was an eternity." A major figure in the unwritten psychiatric history of the Beats, Cowen was in and out of hospitals for anxiety and depression. She killed herself by jumping out her parents' closed sitting room window in February 1962.

It was Cowen, among others, to whom Gregory Corso was referring at a tribute to Ginsberg, when an audience member asked why there were no women among the Beat writers: "There were women, they were there, I knew them, their families put them in institutions, they were given electric shock. In the '50s if you were male you could be a rebel, but if you were female your families had you locked up."* Cowen wrote several poems for Ginsberg, among them "Teacher—Your Body My Kabbalah," but most of her papers were destroyed by her family after her suicide. Over the years, Leo Skir submitted the manuscripts in his possession to Beat-related journals like *Evergreen Review.*—ed.]

---

* From Steven Scobie's account of the Naropa Institute tribute to Ginsberg, July 1994. Quoted in Brenda Knight's *Women of the Beat Generation* (Berkeley, Calif.: Conari Press, 1996).

Teacher—your body my Kabbalah

Rahamim—Compassion
Tiferete—Beauty

The aroma of Mr. Rochesters cigars
among the flowers
       Bursting through
       I am trying to choke you
       Delicate thought
       Posed
       Frankenstein of delicate grace
          posed by my fear
       And you
       Graciously
       Take me by the throat

The body hungers before the soul
       And after thrusts for its own memory

Why not afraid to hurt elig—
    Couldn't hurt me except in wit, in funny
    I couldn't, wouldn't arm in relation
    but with a rose or rather skunk cabbage

Just—Mere come I break through grey paper
     room
       Your
       Frankenstein
What is the word from   Deberoux Babtiste
The Funambule   I

Desnuelu (who's he?)   to choke you
Duhamel   and you
De broille   Graciously
Deberaux   Take me by the throat
Decraux
Barrault
Deberaux
Delicate
French logic
Black daisy chain of nuns
Nous sommes tous assasins
Keith's jumping old man in the waves
                methadrine
        morning dance of delicacy
        "I want you to pick me up
            when I fall down"
                            I wouldn't and fell
                                not even death
                            I waited for
                                stinking
                                with the room
                                like cat shit
                                would take me
Donald's first bed wherein this fantasy
        shame changing him to you
        And you talking of plum blossom scrolls
        and green automobiles
Shame making body thought
        a game
Cat's cradle & imaginary
    lattices of knowledge & Bach
        system

Fearing making guilt making shame
        making fantasy & logic & gave &
        elegance of covering splendour
        emptying memory of the event
        covering splendour with mere elegance
        covering
        sneer between the angels
Wouldn't couldn't
Fear of the killer
    dwarf with the bag of tricks & the colonels picture
To do my killing for me
God *is* hidden
        And not for picture postcards.

Allen Ginsberg and Allen Young

"Accept my soul with all its throbbings and sweetness..."

from an interview in Gay Sunshine, *conducted in 1972 at Ginsberg's Cherry Valley farm in upstate New York*

YOUNG: One of the things that provoked this whole conversation between us was my reading of *The Dharma Bums* last summer. In that book the character Alvah, who is quite obviously you, is portrayed by Kerouac as heterosexual. There are a number of sexual encounters and there isn't any indication that there was any kind of homosexuality in this group of people.

GINSBERG: That was Kerouac's particular shyness. You know, I made it with Kerouac quite often. And Neal, his hero, and I were lovers, also, for many years, from 1946 on, on and off, at least I wanted to be, and we got to bed quite often, we didn't really fully...finally he didn't want any more sex with me, he rejected me! That's what he did! But we were still making it in the mid-1960s after having known each other in the mid-40s, so that's a pretty long, close friendship—Neal and Jack, for that matter.

YOUNG: Did Jack Kerouac identify himself as being a gay person?

GINSBERG: No, he didn't. A lot of that [the incidents described in *The Dharma Bums*] took place in the cottage we all held together [in Berkeley], and then I had been living with Peter for several years. Peter, Jack, Gary [Snyder] and I and various other people were all sleeping with one or two girls that were around. Jack saw me screwing and was astounded at my virility. I guess he decided to write a novel in which I was a big, virile hero instead of a Jewish Communist fag.

—

YOUNG: What was your reaction to that? Did you feel that he was hiding?

GINSBERG: I didn't notice. *On the Road* has one scene in the original manuscript in a motel where Dean Moriarty screws a traveling salesman with whom they ride to Chicago in a big Cadillac; and there's a two line description of it which fills out Cassady's character and gives it dimension. That was eliminated from the book by Malcolm Cowley in the mid-50s, and Jack consented to that. So Jack actually did talk about it a little in his writing.

In a book that's being published now, *Visions of Cody*, there's a longer description of the same scene. It was written in 1950–51 by Kerouac and was his first book after *On the Road,* a sequel to it. It was a great experimental book, including a couple of hundred pages of taped, transcribed conversation between him and Neal, over grass at midnight in Los Gatos or San Jose, talking about life to each other, the first times they got laid, and jacking off, and running around Denver.

YOUNG: Why is it first coming out now?

GINSBERG: Kerouac always wanted it published. But the commercial publishing world wasn't ready for a book of such great looseness and strange genius and odd construction. It's more like a Gertrude Stein *Making of Americans* than it is speedy Kerouac.

YOUNG: Was it a fight for Kerouac to get his stuff published?

GINSBERG: Oh, yeah. *On the Road* was written in 1950 and was never published till '57, even though he had previously published his great book, *Town and the City*. The commercial insistency was that he write something nice and simple so everybody could understand it, to explain what the beat generation was all about. So he wrote *The Dharma Bums,* to order, for his publisher, a sort of exercise in virtuosity and bodhisattva magnanimity. He wrote in short sentences that everybody could understand, describing the spiritual revolution as he saw it, using as a hero Gary Snyder; actually, "Japhy Ryder" is Gary Snyder.

YOUNG: So then your portrayal as a heterosexual doesn't have anything to do with being in the closet.

GINSBERG: No. I came out of the closet at Columbia in 1946. The first person I told about it was Kerouac, cause I was in love with him. He was staying in my room up in the bed, and I was sleeping on a pallet on the floor. I said, "Jack, you know, I love you, and I want to sleep with you, and I really like men." And he said, "Ooooooh, no..." We'd known each other maybe a year, and I hadn't said anything.

At that time Kerouac was very handsome, very beautiful, and mellow—mellow in the sense of infinitely tolerant, like Shakespeare or Tolstoy or Dostoevsky, infinitely understanding. So in a sense—there's a term that I heard Robert Duncan use for poetry and I've heard others use it for relations between guru and disciple—as a slightly older person and someone who I felt had more authority, his tolerance gave me *permission* to open up and talk, you know, cause I felt there was space for me to talk, where he was. He wasn't going to hit me. He wasn't going to reject me, really, he was going to accept my soul with all its throbbings and sweetness and worries and dark woes and sorrows and heartaches and joys and glees and mad understanding of mortality, cause that was the same thing he had. And actually we wound up sleeping together maybe within a year, a couple of times. I blew him, I guess. He once blew me, years later. It was sort of sweet, peaceful.

Jack Kerouac

"If like me you renounce love and the world..."

from a letter to Ginsberg, January 18, 1955

[After falling in love with Peter Orlovsky, Ginsberg wrote to Kerouac, a little anxious about his reaction to the news. Kerouac responded in good spirits, having just been legally released from paying child support for his three-year-old daughter, Jan Michelle Kerouac, on the grounds of his disability from phlebitis.—ed.]

Your long letter about the sad love. If like me you renounce love and the world, you will suffer the sorrows of renunciation, which come in the form of ennui and "what to do, what to dream?" dig. But if you grasp at sadlove, ergo, you suffer from sadlove. I dug whole letter and loved the Dostoevskian bare Neal bumping in [Al] Hinkle in hall (like the time the three of us bumped in Watsonville and had big poker game with brakemen)—Peter O sounds very great and I know that whatever happens, you will know how to reassure the sad heart therein. Be sure to do that, before too late, before disappears. Reassure canuck painter* too. Cut out. Or if not cut out, for how can I know any more than Burroughs deal…at least never recriminate, never sadden others, always be kind and forgive and suffer. I suffer from loneliness, long afternoons after dhyana [meditation], or rather really before, what's there to do? The letter beautiful, I read it line by line in morning, savoring every bit of it, how I love letters

* The painter Robert LaVigne had introduced Ginsberg to his young boyfriend, Peter, and then set them up together. It was not a painless transition.

---

from you my fine sweet Allen. And dont ever worry about me getting mad at you again—I swear off of that for the last last time, every time I get mad at you it later turns out imaginary reasons of dust.

Allen Ginsberg

Malest Cornifici Tuo Catullo

I'm happy, Kerouac, your madman Allen's
finally made it: discovered a new young cat,
and my imagination of an eternal boy
walks on the streets of San Francisco,
handsome, and meets me in cafeterias
and loves me. Ah don't think I'm sickening.
You're angry at me. For all of my lovers?
It's hard to eat shit, without having visions;
when they have eyes for me it's like Heaven.

San Francisco, 1955

Allen Ginsberg

from **Howl**

*For Carl Solomon**

I

I saw the best minds of my generation destroyed by madness, starving
hysterical naked,
dragging themselves through the negro streets at dawn looking for an
angry fix,
angelheaded hipsters burning for the ancient heavenly connection to the
starry dynamo in the machinery of night,
who poverty and tatters and hollow-eyed and high sat up smoking in the
supernatural darkness of cold-water flats floating across the tops of
cities contemplating jazz,
who bared their brains to Heaven under the El and saw Mohammedan
angels staggering on tenement roofs illuminated,
who passed through universities with radiant cool eyes hallucinating
Arkansas and Blake-light tragedy among the scholars of war,
who were expelled from the academies for crazy & publishing obscene
odes on the windows of the skull,
who cowered in unshaven rooms in underwear, burning their money in
wastebaskets and listening to the Terror through the wall,
who got busted in their pubic beards returning through Laredo with a
belt of marijuana for New York,
who ate fire in paint hotels or drank turpentine in Paradise Alley, death,
or purgatoried their torsos night after night

* Although Carl Solomon was not a writer, Ginsberg described him as "an intuitive Bronx dadaist and
prose-poet." They met as patients at the Columbia Psychiatric Institute in 1949. *Howl* is based in part
on Solomon's life, though incidents from Beat legend are everywhere in it.

with dreams, with drugs, with waking nightmares, alcohol and cock and endless balls,

incomparable blind streets of shuddering cloud and lightning in the mind leaping toward poles of Canada & Paterson, illuminating all the motionless world of Time between,

Peyote solidities of halls, backyard green tree cemetery dawns, wine drunkenness over the rooftops, storefront boroughs of teahead joyride neon blinking traffic light, sun and moon and tree vibrations in the roaring winter dusks of Brooklyn, ashcan rantings and kind king light of mind,

who chained themselves to subways for the endless ride from Battery to holy Bronx on benzedrine until the noise of wheels and children brought them down shuddering mouth-wracked and battered bleak of brain all drained of brilliance in the drear light of Zoo,

who sank all night in submarine light of Bickford's floated out and sat through the stale beer afternoon in desolate Fugazzi's, listening to the crack of doom on the hydrogen jukebox,

who talked continuously seventy hours from park to pad to bar to Bellevue to museum to the Brooklyn Bridge,

a lost battalion of platonic conversationalists jumping down the stoops off fire escapes off windowsills off Empire State out of the moon,

yacketayakking screaming vomiting whispering facts and memories and anecdotes and eyeball kicks and shocks of hospitals and jails and wars,

whole intellects disgorged in total recall for seven days and nights with brilliant eyes, meant for the Synagogue cast on the pavement,

who vanished into nowhere Zen New Jersey leaving a trail of ambiguous picture postcards of Atlantic City Hall,

suffering Eastern sweats and Tangerian bone-grindings and migraines of China under junk-withdrawal in Newark's bleak furnished room,

who wandered around and around at midnight in the railroad yard wondering where to go, and went, leaving no broken hearts,

who lit cigarettes in boxcars boxcars boxcars racketing through snow toward
    lonesome farms in grandfather night,
who studied Plotinus Poe St. John of the Cross telepathy and bop kaballa
    because the cosmos instinctively vibrated at their feet in Kansas,
who loned it through the streets of Idaho seeking visionary indian angels
    who were visionary indian angels,
who thought they were only mad when Baltimore gleamed in supernatural
    ecstasy,
who jumped in limousines with the Chinaman of Oklahoma on the
    impulse of winter midnight streetlight smalltown rain,
who lounged hungry and lonesome through Houston seeking jazz or sex
    or soup, and followed the brilliant Spaniard to converse about America
    and Eternity, a hopeless task, and so took ship to Africa,
who disappeared into the volcanoes of Mexico leaving behind nothing
    but the shadow of dungarees and the lava and ash of poetry scattered
    in fireplace Chicago,
who reappeared on the West Coast investigating the F.B.I. in beards
    and shorts with big pacifist eyes sexy in their dark skin passing out
    incomprehensible leaflets,
who burned cigarette holes in their arms protesting the narcotic tobacco
    haze of Capitalism,
who distributed Supercommunist pamphlets in Union Square weeping
    and undressing while the sirens of Los Alamos wailed them down,
    and wailed down Wall, and the Staten Island ferry also wailed,
who broke down crying in white gymnasiums naked and trembling
    before the machinery of other skeletons,
who bit detectives in the neck and shrieked with delight in policecars for
    committing no crime but their own wild cooking pederasty and
    intoxication,
who howled on their knees in the subway and were dragged off the roof
    waving genitals and manuscripts,

who let themselves be fucked in the ass by saintly motorcyclists, and
   screamed with joy,
who blew and were blown by those human seraphim, the sailors, caresses
   of Atlantic and Caribbean love,
who balled in the morning in the evenings in rosegardens and the grass of
   public parks and cemeteries scattering their semen freely to whomever
   come who may [...]

William Burroughs

"I find myself getting jealous of Kiki..."

from a letter to Jack Kerouac, August 18, 1954

I find myself getting jealous of Kiki—he is besieged by importunate queens. In fact I am downright involved, up to my neck in Maya.* He is a sweet kid, and it is so pleasant to loll about in the afternoon smoking tea, sleeping and having sex with no hurry, running leisurely hands over his lean, hard body, and finally we doze off, all wrapped around each other, into the delicious sleep of a hot afternoon in a cool, darkened room, a sleep that is different from any other sleep, a twilight in which I savour, with a voluptuous floating sensation, the state of sleep, feeling the nearness of Kiki's young body, the sweet, imperceptible, drawing together in sleep, leg inching over leg, arm encompassing body, hips hitching closer, stiffening organs reaching out to touch warm flesh.

Jack, I would think twice before giving up sex.** It's a basic kick and when it's good as it can be it's *good*.

* From Hindu philosophy, meaning "illusion."
** Kerouac had made a Buddhist renunciation of sex in April 1954.

Alan Ansen

"The Newport News has arrived in Venice for a week's stay..."

News Item
"The Army gets the medals…"

Tamed by an income, by beauty and the water,
Hemmed in by palaces lighter than air,
By churches that bring a city square to order
And tactfully arrange a scene, a lift,
By hawk-nosed countesses, by leashed leers,
And by an exquisite civility that shames me,
I have reached thirty-five.
I sip my aperitif, go to bed with girls,
Read the Gazzettino, think loyal thoughts,
Attend parties, dress better, live up to but not beyond my means
And hardly ever get beaten up.

But oh ugly Boston ringed with heavenly light,
Where one lone boy, scared by the draft,
Blossomed through lust into the passion of poetry
Taught by sailors that angels are real.
Black eye, bloody nose, dirty old sweater stained with vomit,
Refreshed body graced with come,
Happy mind, rejoicing that its learning could have meaning,
Dancing spirit with its new-found worship.

Venice, I am not just part of your incomparable poem,
I have my own poetry and my own past.
God bless those American angels from the sea

—

For reminding me
"There is one story and one story only."
It promises all and performs nothing
Except to transform existence into life.

William Burroughs

A. J.'s Annual Party

from NAKED LUNCH

On Screen. Red-haired, green-eyed boy, white skin with a few freckles…
kissing a thin brunette girl in slacks. Clothes and hair-do suggest exis-
tentialist bars of all the world cities. They are seated on low bed covered
in white silk. The girl opens his pants with gentle fingers and pulls out
his cock which is small and very hard. A drop of lubricant gleams at its
tip like a pearl. She caresses the crown gently: "Strip, Johnny." He takes
off his clothes with swift sure movements and stands naked before her,
his cock pulsing. She makes a motion for him to turn around and he
pirouettes across the floor parodying a model, hand on hip. She takes off
her shirt. Her breasts are high and small with erect nipples. She slips off
her underpants. Her pubic hairs are black and shiny. He sits down beside
her and reaches for her breast. She stops his hands.

"Darling, I want to rim you," she whispers.

"No. Not now."

"Please, I want to."

"Well, all right. I'll go wash my ass."

"No, I'll wash it."

"Aw shucks now, it aint dirty."

"Yes it is. Come on now, Johnny boy."

She leads him into the bathroom. "All right, get down." He gets
down on his knees and leans forward, with his chin on the bath mat.
"Allah," he says. He looks back and grins at her. She washes his ass with
soap and hot water sticking her finger up it.

"Does that hurt?"

"Noooooooooooo."

"Come along, baby." She leads the way into the bedroom. He lies down on his back and throws his legs back over his head, clasping elbows behind his knees. She kneel down and caress the backs of his thighs, his balls, running her fingers down the perennial divide. She push his cheeks apart, lean down and begin licking the anus, moving her head in a slow circle. She push at the sides of the asshole, licking deeper and deeper. He close his eyes and squirm. She lick up the perennial divide. His small, tight balls…. A great pearl stands out on the tip of his circumcised cock. Her mouth closes over the crown. She sucks rhythmically up and down, pausing on the up stroke and moving her head around in a circle. Her hand plays gently with his balls, slide down and middle finger up his ass. As she suck down toward the root of his cock she tickle his prostate mockingly. He grin and fart. She is sucking his cock now in a frenzy. His body begins to contract, pulling up toward his chin. Each time the contraction is longer. "Wheeeeee!" the boy yell, every muscle tense, his whole body strain to empty through his cock. She drinks his jissom which fills her mouth in great hot spurts. He lets his feet flop back onto the bed. He arches his back and yawns.

Mary is strapping on a rubber penis: "Steely Dan III from Yokohama," she says, caressing the shaft. Milk spurts across the room.

"Be sure that milk is pasteurized. Don't go giving me some kinda awful cow disease like anthrax or glanders or aftosa…."

"When I was a transvestite Liz in Chi used to work as an exterminator. Make advances to pretty boys for the thrill of being beaten as a man. Later I catch this one kid, overpower him with supersonic judo I learned from an old Lesbian Zen monk. I tie him up, strip off his clothes with a razor and fuck him with Steely Dan I. He is so relieved I don't castrate him literal he come all over my bedbug spray."

"What happen to Steely Dan I?"

"He was torn in two by a bull dike. Most terrific vaginal grip I ever experienced. She could cave in a lead pipe. It was one of her parlor tricks."

"And Steely Dan II?"

"Chewed to bits by a famished candiru in the Upper Baboonsasshole. And don't say 'Wheeeeeee!' this time."

"Why not? It's real boyish."

He looks at the ceiling, hands behind the head, cock pulsing. "So what shall I do? Can't shit with that dingus up me. I wonder is it possible to laugh and come at the same time? I recall, during the war, at the Jockey Club in Cairo, me and my asshole buddy, Lu, both gentlemen by acts of Congress...nothing else could have done such a thing to either of us...So we got laughing so hard we piss all over ourselves and the waiter say: 'You bloody hash-heads, get out of here!' I mean, if I can laugh the piss out of me I should be able to laugh out jissom. So tell me something real funny when I start coming. You can tell by certain premonitory quiverings of the prostate gland...."

She puts on a record, metallic cocaine be-bop. She greases the dingus, shoves the boy's legs over his head and works it up his ass with a series of corkscrew movements of her fluid hips. She moves in a slow circle, revolving on the axis of the shaft. She rubs her hard nipples across his chest. She kisses him on neck and chin and eyes. He runs his hands down her back to her buttocks, pulling her into his ass. She revolves faster, faster. His body jerks and writhes in convulsive spasms. "Hurry up, please," she says. "The milk is getting cold." He does not hear. She presses her mouth against his. Their faces run together. His sperm hits her breast with light, hot licks.

Mark is standing in the doorway. He wears a turtle-neck black sweater. Cold, handsome, narcissistic face. Green eyes and black hair. He looks at Johnny with a slight sneer, his head on one side, hands on his jacket pockets, a graceful hoodlum ballet. He jerks his head and Johnny walk ahead of him into the bedroom. Mary follow. "All right, boys," she say, sitting down naked on a pink silk dais overlooking the bed. "Get with it!"

Mark begin to undress with fluid movements, hip-rolls, squirm out of his turtle-neck sweater revealing his beautiful white torso in a mocking belly dance. Johnny deadpan, face frozen, breath quick, lips dry, remove his clothes and drop them on the floor. Mark lets his shorts fall on one foot. He kick like a chorus-girl, sending the shorts across the room. Now he stand naked, his cock stiff, straining up and out. He run slow eyes over Johnny's body. He smile and lick his lips.

Mark drop on one knee, pulling Johnny across his back by one arm. He stand up and throw him six feet onto the bed. Johnny land on his back and bounce. Mark jump up and grab Johnny's ankles, throw his legs over his head. Mark's lips are drawn back in a tight snarl. "All right, Johnny boy." He contracts his body, slow and steady as an oiled machine, push his cock up Johnny's ass. Johnny give a great sigh, squirming in ecstasy. Mark hitches his hands behind Johnny's shoulders, pulling him down onto his cock which is buried to the hilt in Johnny's ass. Great whistles through his teeth. Johnny screams like a bird. Mark is rubbing his face against Johnny's, snarl gone, face innocent and boyish as his whole liquid being spurt into Johnny's quivering body.

A train roar through him whistle blowing…boat whistle, foghorn, sky rocket burst over oily lagoons…penny arcade open into a maze of dirty pictures…ceremonial cannon boom in the harbor…a scream shoots down a white hospital corridor…out along a wide dusty street between palm trees, whistles out across the desert like a bullet (vulture wings husk in the dry air), a thousand boys come at once in outhouses, bleak public school toilets, attics, basements, treehouses, Ferris wheels, deserted houses, limestone caves, rowboats, garages, barns, rubbly windy city outskirts behind mud walls (smell of dried excrement)…

Brion Gysin

from Cut-ups: A Project for Disastrous Success

[The queer polymath Brion Gysin was a friend of Paul Bowles in Tangier in the mid-1950s and had a restaurant there called the Thousand and One Nights, popular with the expatriate crowd. Gysin lost the business days after discovering, inside a ventilator, a hideous charm of seeds, menstrual blood, pubic hair, and other tokens, wrapped in a message to the Jinn of the Hearth: "May Massa Brahim [Brion] leave this house as the smoke leave this fire, never to return." His path had crossed Burroughs's in Tangier, but the men did not take to each other. They met again in Paris in 1958 and soon became close platonic friends and collaborators, sharing an interest in magic, mind control, and gadgetry. Both lived in Madame Rachou's "Beat Hotel" on the rue Git le Coeur. With Gysin, Burroughs pioneered the Cut-Up, a technique for producing randomized but eerily sensible texts.—ed.]

I barely made it to London, where I sold my pictures of the Sahara and then crossed to Paris, which I have lived in off and on for the last thirty years. Ran into grey-green Burroughs in the Place St Michel. "Wanna score?" For the first time in all the years I had known him, I really scored with him.

Hamri and I had first met him in the hired gallery of the Rembrandt Hotel in Tangier in 1954 when he wheeled into our exhibition, arms and legs flailing, talking a mile a minute. We found he looked very Occidental, more Private Eye than Inspector Lee: he trailed long vines of Bannisteria Caapi [yage] from the Upper Amazon after him and old Mexican bull-fight posters fluttered out from under his long trench coat instead of a shirt. An odd blue light often flashed around under the brim of his hat.

Hamri and I decided, rather smugly, that we could not afford to know him because he was too Spanish. Obviously he would soon pick up with Manolo, Pepe, Kiki…whereas; "Henrique!" "Joselito!" Burroughs whinnied—sort of South American boy-cries, for all we knew.

I cannot say I saw Burroughs clear during the restaurant days that followed. Caught a glimpse of him glimmering rapidly along through the shadows from one *farmacia* to the next, hugging a bottle of paregoric. I close my eyes and see him in winter, cold silver blue, rain dripping from the points of his hat and his nose. Willie the Rat scuttles over the purple sheen of wet pavements, sniffing. Burroughs slices through the crowd in the Socco Chico, his raincoat glinting like the underbelly of a shark. He dashes at Kiki with a raised knife of rain-glitter running off his chop-finger hand. Burroughs lives chez Tony Dutch.* He pokes a long, quivering nose out of calle Cristianos, picking up on: Is Kiki around? He plucks Kiki out of the Mar Chica [bar] with his glittering eye. When you squint up your eyes at him, he turns into Coleridge, De Quincy, Poe, Baudelaire and Gide… Now, wherefore stoppest thou me?

Hamri and me we waggle our beards—everything just like we always say. Meester Weeli-yam. (*Weeli, weeli!* What Arab women cry in alarm. Hamri's joke.) Meester Weeli-yam lives in a room Hamri and I know well, and we can imagine him down there, or so we thought, but we never could, really, because we never went to see him in all the years and really could never have imagined the celestial number of empty Eukudol boxes he had stacked up; we never knew. We never heard Kiki say: "Quedase con su medicina, Meester William," and shut the door to go away and be killed by just such another knife. But that was in another country and the boy is dead.**

---

* His rented room at the end of a dark alley off the Socco Chico was attached to a male brothel run by a poodle-owning Dutchman who wore makeup.

** Burroughs's young Spanish boyfriend Kiki, who nursed him through a few attempts to kick his various habits, was later stabbed to death in Spain by a jealous male lover, who had caught him in bed with a woman.

So, when Meester Weeli-yam show in St Michel, I pause; hearing Paul Bowles: "I really don't know; they're all so taken up with madness and drugs. I don't get it. But you'd like Burroughs if only you'd get to know him." We make a meet. He lives in "Heart'sease Street," rue Git le Coeur, where I lived 1938–39. But "Must hurry to my doctor—yes, my analyst; recommended by a rich junky friend with whom I goofed on my apomorphine cure with Dr Dent, unfortunately."* Later, I make it up to room #15. Where are the alumni of room #15 today?

* Despite his relapse, Burroughs argued the benefits of this London doctor's cure for many years to come.

John Giorno

"I Met Jack Kerouac in 1958 for One Glorious Moment..."*

I met Jack Kerouac on May 31, 1958, Saturday night at about nine at a party in New York. It was being struck by lightning, and totally great.

I was 21 years old, just finishing college at Columbia. Classes had ended and graduation was in three days. Alice Dignan, my girl friend and I were drunk, as usual, on vodka martinis. We hated parties, but Alice had heard from Carl Andre that a cool party was going to happen at 108th and West End Avenue. I was gay and the local famous poet; young, beautiful, and it got me what I wanted and all I wanted to do was sex and ready for anything; rich enough, my family gave me an allowance and paid my credit cards. Alice and I were a famous couple, small consolation for our suffering, and our egos were all that we had. We were obnoxious.

We arrived as dysfunctional royalty. Alice was wearing a black cocktail dress, and I, a rumpled white linen suit. We walked through the hot crowded party with the arrogant disdain of cats, scanning everything, but not looking at anything, nothing was worthy. We believed that being completely outrageous, burned away ignorance, that being completely over the top, destroyed delusion and dualist concepts. Crazy wisdom was absolute liberation.

We walked through several rooms of the large West End apartment, where people stood holding drinks, smoking and talking. We nodded occasionally, and headed toward the kitchen where the bar was. We ran into someone we knew, and were relieved there was someone to talk to. We moved on, and stood dumbly in a dim crowded hallway, drinking red wine and smoking Camels.

* From his memoir-in-progress. Giorno is a Beat-influenced gay poet/performer who founded Dial-a-Poem in New York, produced hundreds of innovative spoken-word recordings for Giorno Poetry Systems, and starred in Warhol's first film, the seven-hour-long study of a sleeping man called *Sleep* (1964), which nearly caused riots on its initial screenings.

—

"There's Allen Ginsberg," said Alice. I didn't understand. "John, darling, there is Allen Ginsberg… The one you really like, who wrote Howl!"

"Where?" I said, looking around and not seeing. Allen Ginsberg was standing behind me with his shoulder poking into my back, talking to someone. I was stunned. My hero poet, who existed only in myth, was touching me. I had read Howl in 1956, two years before; and it had completely changed my life. I was speechless.

"Hello, Allen," said Alice, extending her hand grandly. He bowed and kissed it, like a gentleman. "My name is Alice Dignan…and this is John Giorno." She was obviously deferring to me, to attract Allen. "He's a poet."

Allen got interested. "You're a poet? Who are your teachers?"

"I had them all. And they weren't altogether that good. They were wonderful, but a big waste of time or a small waste of time."

"How can you say that!" said Allen disapprovingly.

This was not what Allen wanted to hear. I was surprised at his being so straight. But I wanted him to like me and I would have done anything. "They are great!" I said enthusiastically. "And I've had them all. Mark Van Doren, Lionel Trilling, Moses Hadas, Eric Bentley, and Alan Watts. They are all great. They changed my life." I was shameless. I was really hustling him. And I said boldly, "I am editor of the Columbia Review. Or I was." I laughed gently. "Impermanence."

"Wow!… You are!" said Allen, almost predictably impressed. I was quickly getting to know him.

We talked about Mark Van Doren, who I really liked, and Allen knew. "But that's all finished. I'm at the moment of being liberated. Just now, this coming Tuesday, I graduate Columbia College. I've always been a student, going endlessly to classes. Now, I'm a free man, finally, a freeman." Allen seemed charmed.

Someone came up and asked Allen something, and distracted him.

"You're in luck," Alice whispered. I didn't understand. "He likes boys. You are in luck, John, darling!" I was offended and hurt, as I was secretly gay, nobody talked about it, and it was mean of her to say that.

—

Allen turned his attention back to me, and said, "What are your plans?"

"I'm a poet. I just want to write. I'm just going to work on poems."

Someone else interrupted. Thin Peter Orlovsky bounced up and down. Then I realized standing with us was Gregory Corso; and Jack Kerouac was standing behind me, leaning his head over my shoulder, listening to us.

I was stunned speechless. Jack Kerouac, my poet god, was right here. I had read *On the Road, The Subterraneans,* and *Dharma Bums.* I really dug him. I got dizzy, a blissful rush in my head and heart palpitations. For an instant, I was in a god world; dumb struck.

After a while, I managed to say something to Allen, "What year were you here at Columbia?"

"1948," said Allen, being exact.

"This is '58."

"And Jack was 1944... At our first meeting Jack offered me a beer over breakfast, and when I said, 'No, no. Discretion is the better part of valor,' Jack barked back, 'Awe, where's my food!' "

Everyone laughed a little awkwardly. Jack Kerouac smiled warmly at Allen. Jack was so beautiful. He was wearing a dark blue button short-sleeve shirt, and had an amazingly handsome face, magnetizing and attracting.

"Oh, you went to school here?" I said daringly, leaning my shoulder toward Jack. I had to say something to him, I loved him. "I just finished, now. I'm being released from the suffering of school."

Jack Kerouac leaned forward with his thumb stuck in his belt and his hand touched me, and he said, "You're lucky."

I was thrilled, I couldn't believe he said those words, a rush of joy. Then, Jack leaned forward again, and said something else. It was very noisy and I couldn't hear him. How could I not hear what Jack Kerouac said to me. A moment of panic. His lips touched my ear and I could ear sound, but I couldn't understand the words. For an instant, we looked into each other's eyes, our hearts hooked together through our eyes, bliss and clarity, beyond concepts.

—

I asked him something stupid, just to continue being connected with him. The party was very noisy and he couldn't hear me. He put his ear touching my lips. And as we were drunk and staggering, our cheeks brushed and bumped against each other. I got an electric shock. We could have kissed; but there were so many people.

I said something stupid and he smiled, and said something. He was so beautiful. I was so excited. I still couldn't quite hear what he was saying, but I was in love with the smell of his body, his heat and compassion radiating from his heart.

"Why are we here?" said Jack.

"I don't know." Looking in his eyes, I felt dumb and frightened. It was the right answer. The defeat of ignorance, that included the possibility of the mind resting in primordial purity, beyond answers, miraculously.

Gregory Corso said something loudly. He handed a joint to Jack, who took a puff, and passed it to me. I inhaled long and deep, held it in my lungs, and passed the joint back to Jack. I was ecstatic, smoking marijuana with Jack Kerouac. In 1958, Jack was a virtual god, plus he looked like Marlon Brando on the Waterfront as Julius Caesar. It was a very hot night. I was hyperventilating, and sweat poured from me in sheets.

Allen Ginsberg was very shrewdly watching us, taking it all in, and disapproving. He stepped forward, pushed between Jack and me, and moved deliberately to cut us off. He broke it up. "Oh! You two know each other!" said Allen, slightly peeved. He separated Jack and me, distracted Jack's attention, and broke the connection.

"Oh no, what is he doing?" I froze and my heart sank.

"Let's go!" Allen led Jack away. They all walked out, moved on, departed, and it was over. They vanished. I was in bewilderness. Happy beyond belief, at such an amazing thing.

"John, darling. Do you feel empty, now that they're gone," said Alice, puffing a cigarette.

"I feel totally great! I felt totally exhilarated! I can't believe that just happened!" It struck me as a good omen, a very auspicious sign, meeting

—

110

these guys, at the moment of the beginning of the rest of my life. I had no idea what I was going to do, but write, and work with poems and poetry, and be a poet.

• • •

Addendum: Little did I know that Allen Ginsberg breaking up Jack Kerouac and me was a sign of things to come. The first of many times that Allen would be an obstacle to me. An endlessly recurring pattern, that went on for forty years, until Allen died, and afterwards. Allen was a good friend on the surface, and a secretly obstructing force; paranoid, but true. Among the many reasons and complicated karma were that Allen was jealous of anyone close to William Burroughs and I lived with William for three decades in the Bunker at 222 Bowery in New York and in Lawrence, Kansas, and toured performing with him endlessly.

I ran into Jack Kerouac occasionally during his brief visits to New York over the next ten years, until he died in 1969. He became a nice, overweight, drunk guy. Nothing ever happened again, because it was too much trouble to make it happen. I had gone on to Andy Warhol and the 1960s, and the golden age of promiscuity.

John Wieners

A Poem for Cocksuckers

[The Boston poet John Wieners was a wunderkind whose first book, *The Hotel Wentley Poems* (1958), was written in six days of heartache while he lived in a crummy residential hotel of the same name in San Francisco. Out of the closet from the age of sixteen, Wieners spent time in mental hospitals, that crucible of postwar writers. He was a friend of Ginsberg, Michael McClure, and other Beat poets, and had worked with the Poet's Theatre at Harvard, where he impressed Frank O'Hara—in part by wearing eye shadow in public—and studied with Charles Olson at Black Mountain College. The Wentley poems made Wieners famous in the small way of American poetry. "The whole book is the work of a naked flower," wrote Ginsberg, "a tragic clown, doomed sensibility, absolutely REAL, no more self pity." *—ed.]

Well we can go
in the queer bars w/
our long hair reaching
down to the ground and
we can sing our songs
of love like the black mama
on the juke box, after all
what have we got left.

On our right the faeries
giggle in their lacquered

* Quoted in Neeli Cherkovski's wonderful celebration of the rebel tradition in postwar American verse, *Whitman's Wild Children* (San Francisco: Lapis Press, 1988).

voices & blow
smoke in your eyes let them
it's a nigger's world
and we retain strength.
Our gifts do not desert us,
fountains do not dry
up there are rivers running,
there are mountains
swelling for spring to cascade.

    It is all here between
the powdered legs &
painted eyes of the fairy
friends who do not fail us
        in our hour of
            despair. Take not
away from me the small fires
I burn in the memory of love.

6.20.58

Harold Norse

from Memoirs of a Bastard Angel

[The poet and traveler Harold Norse lived in the "Beat Hotel" in Paris for three years while Burroughs was in residence, and was the first to apply the cut-up method to a novel. He was an early lover of Chester Kallman (W. H. Auden's companion), friend of Tennessee Williams and James Baldwin. He once declined the honor of taking the gawky adolescent Allen Ginsberg's virginity. In the 1970s, he wrote straight erotica with Charles Bukowski for *Hustler*, while writing some of the most memorable protest poetry in the gay liberation movement. Although elderly and infirm, he has spent the last several years working on a massive history of homophobia in literature, from early Christianity to the present.—ed.]

Gaït Frogé threw a party for me, attended mostly by writers and painters, including Corso, his girl friend Jean Campbell (the Campbell soup heiress), Allen Ginsberg, Peter Orlovsky, and my rich boyfriend Tom Donovan (name changed), who supplied the champagne...

Peter Orlovsky, stoned on hashish, sidled over. "Take off your clothes," he said. I glanced nervously at Allen, who stiffened. "Come on," urged Peter. "I wanna see you naked. I wanna blow you." Allen blanched. Friendships have ended for less. "Sorry, Peter, I'm not stoned enough." "*Get* stoned," he said. Straight friends egged me on, yelling, "Take it off! We wanna watch Peter suck it!" I smoked more hash and guzzled more Pfeiffer-Heidsieck. Peter slipped out of his sandals, dropped his jeans, and stood naked. As I peeled I heard Gait mutter to her lover, Norman Rubington, "Now we know. Short and thick, like the rest of him." There was a burst of laughter. I reddened. "It's not short," I said. "It's shy."

More laughter. "I'll be right back," said Peter, heading for the bathroom. "Don't go away—I wanna see it grow." Allen stood up, stripped, and drew applause; after all, he started the Beat myth of public nudity. He planted himself like a sentry before the bathrooom door and crossed his arms on his chest, bristling. His body language spoke loud and clear: "There will be no blow job tonight!" Some men, followed by several women, stripped and soon everyone, except for Corso and Jean Campbell, was dancing nude. Peter emerged and ignored me, for which I was grateful. Allen relaxed. I was relieved.

III.

Queer Shoulder to the Wheel

For Jack Kerouac, it said everything about American culture—and his own long-suffering Beat destiny—that the paperback rights for John Clellon Holmes's Beat-themed novel *Go* sold for $20,000, at the same time that he was offered only a thousand dollars from Ace for *On the Road*.* The real thing wasn't wanted, but the second-hand version was easy money, even when filtered through Holmes's stuffy intellectualism and stabs at hipster nonchalance. The commercial exploitation of the Beats was just beginning. It took six years for *On the Road* to find a publisher, but when it did appear, in September 1957, it was an immediate best seller and went into a second printing within two weeks. Audiences who flocked to *Rebel without a Cause* burned to read the Beat manifesto, or at least carry a copy. The zeitgeist had made way for Kerouac, his path cleared—and complicated—by Ginsberg's notoriety as well as by the emerging fascination with the Beats. Oliver Harris, who would edit Burroughs's letters, described the Beats as "the first writers born in the spotlight of the modern media." By 1959, there would be a book on Beat culture, a Rent-a-Beatnik service advertised in the *Village Voice*, and the first television Beatnik, the sensitive, turtleneck-wearing Maynard G. Krebs on *Dobie Gillis.* Soon the embarrassing film versions of Kerouac's books would begin to appear, as if to cancel out the Beats' tentative admission to the canon in Donald Allen's groundbreaking 1960 anthology *New American Poetry: 1945-1960*.

* The deal fell through, and the book was later published by Viking.

Their inclusion in the Allen anthology was big news to the Beats (Ferlinghetti's *A Coney Island of the Mind* would go on to become the best-selling poetry book of the 1960s), but they barely registered the CBS television series *Route 66* (1960–1964), with its suspiciously familiar premise of two hipsters who drove restlessly across the country in search of kicks.

As a former girlfriend, Joyce Johnson, wrote of Kerouac's sudden fame: "Thousands were waiting for a prophet to liberate them from the cautious middle-class lives they had been reared to inherit." He was interviewed on television talk shows and for countless articles. People approached him on the street, in bars. He kept his phone off the hook. Joyce Johnson intercepted one proposition from a desperate woman who explained that while Joyce was young the caller was already twenty-nine years old: "I've got to fuck him now, before it's too late."

But reaction against the Beats was profound, and Kerouac took it personally.* A typical article in *Time* dubbed Ginsberg "the discount-house Whitman of the Beat Generation" and Kerouac "the latrine laureate of Hobohemia," then described the Beats in general as "a pack of oddballs who celebrate booze, dope, sex and despair." Norman Podheretz, who would prove a wily and long-lived opponent, argued in *Esquire* in December 1958 that the Beat writers had "been advertised as the spokesmen for all the hipsters, all the junkies and all the juvenile delinquents in America—as though it were some kind of special virtue to speak for a vicious tendency." To confuse matters, the media conflated the serious writers and artists of the movement with all their beard- and sandal-wearing adherents. "What offered itself as an intellectual refreshment has turned out to be little more than unwashed eccentricity," wrote John Ciardi in 1960. Even friends of the Beats, like Carl Solomon, could make easy fun of the movement. In a short essay called "Suggestions to Improve the Public Image of the Beatnik," he reflected that "it is most

* As did his enemies. As late as the 1980s, Norman Podheretz—that unlikely heir to the Puritans—protested the opening of a Kerouac memorial in the writer's hometown of Lowell, Massachusetts.

important now to change the smell of the Beatnik. Instead of using, for example, the word 'shit' so often in their poems, I suggest that they tactfully substitute 'roses' wherever the other word appears."

Kerouac found himself attacked by critics, yet offered thousands of dollars to write for *Playboy*. Always a heavy drinker, he climbed into his "liquid armor," retreating into week-long binges and reactionary rants. When *Big Sur* (1962), the story of his mental breakdown, flopped with the New York literary establishment, Kerouac set out on a twenty-day bar crawl of his hometown of Lowell, Massachusetts, raging that the Jews had kept him down. Between the 1950s stereotypes of the degenerate Beatnik and the left-wing protests of the 1960s, Kerouac felt that his message had been hopelessly obscured: there was neither reverence nor goodness in characters like Ken Kesey's Merry Pranksters, who dishonored the flag. The "rucksack revolution" Kerouac prophesied in *The Dharma Bums* (1958) had come to pass. Throughout the 1960s, young people were dropping out of the cycle of "work, produce, consume, work, produce, consume" that he had lamented, and taking to the road. But instead of the Zen lunacy and spontaneous versifying that he had hoped for, Kerouac saw lawlessness and Communism in the hippie movement. In later years, he kept a stack of *National Review* magazines near his reading chair.

Ginsberg and Burroughs were thicker-skinned, enjoying the adulation and shrugging off the attacks. Since their first soft-focus boy fantasies, they knew that they'd never be fully accepted. With his royalties from *Naked Lunch*, Burroughs was able to work for years on cut-ups and fold-ins, film and tape projects, and calligraphic drawings, few of which had commercial value. Afraid that there were active warrants for his arrest on a variety of drug charges, he remained outside the United States until the mid-1960s, missing the Beatnik years and the soul-deadening first surge of Beat fame. As the hipster aesthetic of the postwar years blended into the hippie movement, Ginsberg's preoccupations became those of the counterculture at large, and he assumed his iconic status as a chanting pacifist, drug enthusiast, and corrupter of youth. He proved to be "irreproachably immune to the rewards held out to tractable, commercial, or socially decorative bohemians," as Jane Kramer put it.* "The thing that I've learned from Allen," Michael McClure told an early writer on the Beats, "is social commitment."**

Despite his commitment, Ginsberg could be childlike and gauche, and his lack of inhibition did not always open doors. He was curiously unable to see things from the perspective of power, as in his guileless letter to Defense Secretary Robert McNamara during the Vietnam War, in which he tried to explain that the war was an illusion: "you must by now have read basic Buddhist or Bob Dylan heard, texts & advices how to escape from the trap." He was expelled from both Czechoslovakia and Cuba—in the former instance, for the incriminating contents of a "stolen" notebook that ended up with police, and in the latter for espousing the cause of Cuban queers on television and telling a reporter he had sexual fantasies about Che Guevara.

His organizational prowess, though, was legendary. In a poem for *Woodstock Journal*, Diane di Prima described being called by a journalist for a quote about Gregory Corso, who had (wrongly) been reported as dead. She told him to call Allen Ginsberg's office: "Allen will still have an office after we're all gone and that office will always have quotes for everything."

While Kerouac was politically naïve and suspicious—and not a little disturbed by the ripples he had unwittingly sent out into the culture—Ginsberg seems to have figured out very early that the critical issue of his time was free speech. Any social change was possible if it could only dare to speak its name. Even after the major censorship battles of the late 1950s and 1960s had been won with his help, Ginsberg continued to push for more openness. When the topic of homosexuality arose with journalists, he would often smoothly shift the emphasis to free speech:

* Kramer, 13.
** Quoted in Miles, 212.

—

"I think it's pretty shameful that in this culture people have to be so frightened of their own normal sex lives and frightened of other people knowing about it to the point where they have to go slinking around making ridiculous tragedies of their lives. So...it's necessary for the poets to speak out directly about intimate matters, if they come into the poetry, which they do in mine, and not attempt to hide them or evade the issues."*

Much later, in the 1990s, Ginsberg drew fire for his defense of NAMBLA, the advocacy group for man–boy love, but made it clear that he saw the controversy surrounding the group as a free speech issue: "Attacks on NAMBLA stink of politics, witchhunting for profit, humorlessness, anger, and ignorance." But then he added, with typical candor: "I'm a member of NAMBLA because I love boys too—everybody does, who has a little humanity."

A 1965 photo of Neal Cassady shaving at Ginsberg's San Francisco apartment in 1965 shows a flyer pinned to the bathroom mirror, with line drawings of a nude man and woman, reading "Clothed or NUDE: we are NOT OBSCENE." After the Los Angeles poetry reading at which he'd taken off his clothes to demonstrate to a heckler that the Beat writers wanted "nakedness," Ginsberg had adopted frequent semipublic nudity as a reinforcement of his message. He stripped as a gesture of friendliness, as a defensive move, as an example for others, as a provocation. A Berkeley resident named John Knudsen remembers being at a party with Ginsberg at someone's cottage, when Ginsberg suddenly stood and shucked off his clothes. A nearby coed bolted from her chair, ran to the door, and vomited into the bushes.

The Beat ideals of spontaneity, nakedness, and openness to experience are all related, of course, and were as perfect a contrast to 1950s repression and Cold War jitters as if they stood opposite them on a color

---

* Quoted in Alfred G. Aronowitz's "Portrait of a Beat," *Nugget,* October 1960.

wheel. When John Ciardi railed against the "narcissistic sickliness" of Beat writing, he meant, in part, the frankness of their mostly autobiographical writings, but also "this insistence on the holiness of the impromptu and…the urge to play the lunatic."* *Not* to revise was to be naked before the reader. Spontaneous prose and poetry is not always the most powerful literature—reams and reams of Beat poetry, in particular, are unreadable now—but the practice of spontaneity and nakedness, of freely speaking and writing whatever crossed the mind, was life-altering. It required a change in perspective crucial to all the social movements of the 1960s: an attempt to shift authority from some outside force to one's own feelings and experience. And then, naturally, one wanted different experiences, wilder experiences. This is what Corso meant when he declared in 1975, "We brought about change without a single drop of blood!"

The Beats were sexually subversive not only because of what they wrote, but because sex was woven through their existence. It was not something (or someone) they slipped into behind closed doors but an integral part of their professional activities and public image. Unlike Paul and Jane Bowles, for example (included here as Beat-associated gay writers), the Beats had little sense of a private life. Why hide something as spiritual and universal as sex? Ginsberg, in particular, "was the apostle of a truly visionary sexuality," as Camille Paglia wrote for *Salon.* "Like the expansive, sensual, democratic Whitman,…he saw the continuity between great nature and the human body, bathed in waves of cosmic energy."

Being an apostle of love had its benefits. Ginsberg's sex life began with a frenzy of guilt and self-doubt in the 1940s and gradually mellowed—through the orgies, the girls shared with Peter Orlovsky or Gary Snyder, the loving, musical-bed households he established—to a serene acceptance of his own trade value. When he taught, he didn't feel he was

* John Ciardi, "Epitaph for the Dead Beats," *Saturday Review,* Feb. 6, 1960.

really connecting with a class until he'd had sex with a few of the male students. He would proposition young men who came to his readings and public appearances, frankly asking them to bed, even if they were with their girlfriends. John Giorno, who often performed at the same events, recalls the shock that would cross the faces of these straight boys, followed by a look of wonder: "This is Allen Ginsberg!" As often as not, they would agree to go back to Ginsberg's hotel: "And whether it was because of his candor, or how affectionate he was, they always seemed okay the next day. They'd show up at breakfast with him."*

William Burroughs was far more retiring. Giorno, who had sex with him a few times, remembered him saying, "Why would anyone want me? I look like a victim of Bergen Belsen." "He would never take advantage of his fame the way Ginsberg did," Giorno asserts. "He was so well-mannered."** Despite his reserve, and his lingering discomfort with sex, Burroughs had no trouble admiring a young man's form. In the 1980s, Ira Silverberg heard him exclaim over a boy Ginsberg was seeing: "Look at him. His skin is like *alabaster*."

In 1974, Burroughs returned to the States to find that his hipster street creds were at their most pungent in New York. Ginsberg had found him a lucrative teaching gig and also surrendered—with some regret—the company of a young man named James Grauerholz, who became Burroughs's boyfriend for a few weeks, and then his secretary and close friend.*** The poet and singer Patti Smith announced his return on stage one night: "Mr. Burroughs is back in town. Isn't that great?" With Grauerholz's help, Burroughs discovered he could attract big, adoring crowds for his readings and performances. He was a gay punk hero and a decorated veteran of the war against Control.

He viewed his writing as political. "I do definitely mean what I say to be taken literally," he said of his *Nova* trilogy. "Yes, to make people

---

* Interview with the editor of this volume, October 2003.
** Ibid.
*** Their partnership lasted past Burroughs's death. Grauerholz is his literary executor and at work on a definitive biography.

aware of the true criminality of our times, to wise up the marks. All of my work is directed against those who are bent, through stupidity or design, on blowing up the planet or rendering it uninhabitable."* His way was not the olive branch. In the 1960s, when Ginsberg was organizing demonstrations at which hippies handed out flowers to the glowering Berkeley police, Burroughs countered, "The only way I'd like to see cops given flowers is in a flower pot from a high window."**

Ira Silverberg, who was James Grauerholz's boyfriend in the 1980s, remarks that Burroughs was recognized as a gay forebear, though "it was a peculiar canonization. He was anti-P.C. when the movement was becoming mainstream and P.C."***

> William was a political writer to some extent, but not someone whose concerns were ever representative of a specific political group. He didn't give a shit about gay politics, per se. The more banal issues like domestic partnership didn't come up a lot. William really owned that outsider status, that right not to cave to bourgeois standards. So he had iconographic status as the commercialization of the homo came on. He was the antithesis of all that.†

Neither he nor Ginsberg was interested in identity politics or in any of the pragmatic stances of the increasingly assimilationist gay rights movement. Like the homophile movement of the 1950s, it was simply too narrow a vision to engage them. In one of his few public statements on gay rights,‡ the essay "Sexual Conditioning," Burroughs began with

---

* Miles, 145.
** Ibid., 172.
*** Critic Jamie Russell argues that Burroughs's "un-ironic, masculine model of gay identity…is too problematic and reactionary to be easily negotiated" and that this explains his near-exclusion from the gay literary canon. *Queer Burroughs* (New York: Palgrave, 2001), 131.
† Interview with the editor of this volume, December 2003.
‡ If we don't read his entire oeuvre in this light.

—

righteous indignation but soon veered away to his pet topics of gadgetry and control.

What fascinated Burroughs was the emerging plague. Already prone to paranoia, he saw it as an attempt by the government or the Christian right-wing to get rid of homosexuals and drug users. It was no secret that sex was dangerous. As he told his friend Victor Bockris—before the epidemic—"many sexual myths involve one or both persons being killed. Our sexual feelings make us vulnerable. How many people have been ruined by a sex partner? Sex does provide a point of invasion."* He had contracted Kaposi's Sarcoma earlier (not as a result of HIV), so the peculiar forms of the disease hit home. The whole AIDS phenomenon was eerily reminiscent of the viral themes of his novels. "He thought it was a brilliant way to introduce a pathogen to a community," says Silverberg. "You could create a world-wide plague in one New York sex club."

So while Kerouac moved back in with his mother in the 1960s and married the sister of a childhood friend, and Ginsberg reigned through the hippie years, it was the 1980s and 1990s—with their contracting freedoms and sinister global plots—that would be the era of William Burroughs, the darkest of the three Beat angels.

During the 1960s-1970s, the period in which most of the pieces in this section were written, the Beats were becoming increasingly established in the public eye. What had been an elite group (Diane di Prima speculated that there were maybe fifty to a hundred hipsters—Beats included—in downtown New York in the mid-1950s) was now the geographically dispersed but potent core of a major cultural movement. The Beats' influence has been compared to incense: you can smell it in the air, even if you can't always find the stick. Impossible to imagine Yoko Ono and John Lennon holding press conferences from their hotel bed in 1969 to protest the Vietnam War without the example of both Ginsberg's 1967

* Victor Bockris, *With William Burroughs* (New York: St. Martins, 1996), 185.

"Be In" in San Francisco, and his peace activism at the 1968 Chicago Democratic Convention.

The better-known Beats were fêted and photographed and interviewed like film celebrities (there are excerpts here from both Burroughs's and Ginsberg's *Paris Review* interviews), and whatever they wrote, no matter how slight or fragmentary, was snapped up for publication. Thanks in part to the underground press, like Ed Sanders's Beat-associated *Fuck You*, marginal work like Peter Orlovsky's loopy description of giving Allen a handjob could be published before the tissue dried. This kind of immediacy further blurred the line between public and private. Beat lives and ideas seeped into film and the visual arts, fashion, the New Journalism, education, the poetry revival (still ongoing in the Beat-inspired spoken word movement), the surge of interest in eastern religion and yoga, and fed the drug culture and the rising culture of protest. They were not only famous themselves—role models for personal freedom and expanded consciousness—but had tremendous effect on pop icons like Lennon (who changed the spelling of the "Beetles" in homage to the Beats) and Bob Dylan, who in turn influenced millions.

Around the time of the *Naked Lunch* censorship trials, we find a sly reference in Ginsberg's work to the asshole sandwich of his early poem "In Society." Once signifying his disgust with carnality and gay sex, the image is transformed through acceptance: the same process by which the Beats grew into their daring early ideas and were able to reach so many readers over the next fifty years.

A naked lunch is natural to us,
we eat reality sandwiches.
But allegories are so much lettuce.
Don't hide the madness.

Peter Orlovsky

Me & Allen

Realize big difference between me & Allen—he
has such far verbal poetry image—
connecting images getting sap
realization that leads up
ladder to highness of realization—
    I get high thro feeling
& feelings to more purer
feelings or some thing
like it. —it all takes
place in my torso stomache
& up to chest—got by
long talks with myself—but based not on deep
realization on verbal level
but I get realization on emotions pull—pull of
emotion—emotional sap
juce spreding thro out
body& makes me wigle in
joy—but the set back on
stage of my mind picture
big drips of sadness—sadness
drips—sadness comes forward
& pours buckets from
joints of connecting bone
brain drops into chest
void—chest void passes
it to it into stomache
stage void—tears

flow—bloody tears
flow in to void—
void of tears of Peters
tears based on knowing
void expainding in my
family members that
I've watched over years
but only come to feel
more sharply now—
death in rage handing out
rage to each member heart
face of my famiely—
my famiely disapears cause
heart turns hard & cant
expand into universe
of all time heart—all
big time heart (everybody)
thumping—thumping sadness
into my heart sadness—
no ladder across the heart
no ladder comming out of heart
just a nedle out
of heart jabing rib—
crying pain voice alive—
all day on all days—

September 10, 1958
NYC

Peter Orlovsky

Peter Jerking Allen Off (First Sex Experiment)

[Orlovsky, Ginsberg, Corso, and Burroughs—then together in Tangier—were supposed to be interviewing each other on world politics for a new City Lights magazine called *Journal for the Protection of All Beings*. Irritated by Burroughs's misogyny, then in full flower, Orlovsky opted to "emphasize his commitment to love in the face of Bill and his gang"* by transcribing a lovemaking session between himself and Ginsberg. Several of these transcriptions were made. Some record the lovers' wistful postcoital conversations, in which Ginsberg confided his terror of never having a child, and his fears about aging: "I guess you get disgusted when you realize what male potbellied being you wound up with for wife."—ed.]

AG: I feel horney. Ya better close the windows & the door otherwise it will be chilley & put on a robe. How are you going to jerk me off & do that typing at the same time or lay next to my body?

PO: That's a problem, we did it once already, we have all the time in the world, no rush, I'll use my right hand frist & type with left hand as best I can. OK?

AG: Uhha, Allen gives a sigh of pleasure. That's not if you can keep that up.

PO: I continue jerking him off, his cock has a slight bend, as if a little warped—got that way when allen was fucking a spadechick, the girl

* Miles, 288–89.

—

moved her box just when allen was goig to come so that his cock came out of her cunt and ramed up against some bone above or below her cunt, when it happened it wasent too painful because—I am jerking him off all this time, he puts his hand to mine to make it go faster and puts his other hand into under my robe lays that hand atop my cock—lifts his legs like woman getting screwed and spreads them—takes the ashtrey from little tabol next to bed with my cig drags a puff—puts it out fast—it was

AG: Keep going pettey, don't break the rythum

PO: he will be coming soon—he lifts his legs—lifts his body off bed ass behind part—I keep jerking him off & try to go faster—with rythum—sexey hotter that way

AG: ouch,

PO: am I herting you?

AG: yeaha, yr doing it so irregurlly—hold my balls

PO: he goes to grab my left hand, wants me to hold his balls—so I do

AG: I keep getting hot then all of a sudden it stops—its all so irregular—

PO: I go to stick my finger in his ass hole, figureing that this will get him hot—on the top of his cock—the lips start to usher up a little due drops of pre-expecting joy that seems about to come—I took my left hand now to jerk him off & with right hand fingered his ass hole—the due started to get more deweer, the cock harder—he raised his legs higher into the air as I started to go faster with my hand over his cock now—figureing if he dident come now he might not come because his cock might be

—

getting sore by all this irregular jerking on his cock—starting to come—
the come comes & flies out between wet lips like silver dragon flies &
lands on white sheet—some come falls on his cock & some on my
knuckles, as hes coming I say "at a boy" & he says in responce to that—
a few seconds latter "thats great" & hugs me with both arms & gives
maney a sigh. All over & wiped up come. It took 5:45 am to 6:10 am—
calendar to keep track of how many cigs I smoke in a day & just before
putting my hand to Allens cock I lit a cig & noted it & time when
took. End of jerkoff secsson.

Tangers, 1961

Allen Ginsberg

Why Is God Love, Jack?

Because I lay my
    head on pillows,
Because I weep in the
    tombed studio
Because my heart
    sinks below my navel
because I have an
    old airy belly
  filled with soft
    sighing, and
  remembered breast
    sobs—or
 a hands touch makes
    tender—
Because I get scared—
Because I raise my
    voice singing to
      my beloved self—
Because I do love thee
    my darling, my
    other, my living
      bride
my friend, my old lord
    of soft tender eyes—
Because I am in the
    Power of life & can
    do no more than

submit to the feeling
that I am the One
Lost
Seeking still seeking the
thrill—delicious
bliss in the
heart abdomen loins
& thighs
Not refusing this
38 yr. 145 lb. head
arms & feet of meat
Nor one single Whitmanic
toenail condemn
nor hair prophetic banish
to remorseless Hell,
Because wrapped with machinery
I confess my ashamed desire.

1963

William Burroughs

Sexual Conditioning

The whole area of sex is still shrouded in mystery and ignorance. Any attempt to apply objective experimental methods to the study of sexual phenomena has been firmly discouraged. People who do not think of themselves as religious—doctors, sociologists, psychiatrists—are still thinking in terms laid down by the Christian Church. The church assumes that any sexual activity except intercourse with a legal spouse is absolutely wrong because the Bible says so. They condemn so-called deviant behavior in the strongest terms. Psychiatrists, substituting the word "sick" for "wrong," follow the old Christian line. Recent experiments with electrical brain stimulation, however, has provided a much more precise means of conditioning than psychoanalysis and psychotherapy.

Admittedly, a homosexual can be conditioned to react sexually to a woman, or to an old boot for that matter. In fact, both homo- and heterosexual experimental subjects *have* been conditioned to react sexually to an old boot, and you can save a lot of money in that way.

In the same way, heterosexual males can be conditioned to react sexually to other men. Who is to say that one is more desirable than the other? Who is competent to lay down sexual dogmas and impose them on others? The latter-day apologists of St. Paul who call themselves psychiatrists have little to recommend them but their bad statistics. They couldn't get away with statistics like that in any other line of business. Suppose you run a business and the traffic department isn't getting the consignments out. They say they need more money and more personnel, and the situation gets worse. Consignments stack up like patients in a state hospital. They say they need yet more money and more personnel to cope with the evergrowing traffic problem. How long before you fire the entire traffic department and get someone in there who can do the job? Psychiatrists say they need more money and personnel to deal with the ever-growing problem of mental illness, and the more money and personnel that is channeled into this bottomless pit, the higher the statistics on mental illness climb. Personally I think that mental illness is largely a psychiatric invention.

On December 3rd, 1973, the American Psychiatric Association decided that homosexuality would no longer be considered a mental deviation. Well, if they have more mental patients now than they can handle, it would seem to be a step in the right direction to remove homosexuals from this category. But the decision has caused a storm of protest. One psychiatrist compared the decision to "a psychiatric Watergate which we hope won't be our Waterloo..." They just don't like to see any prospective patients escaping; it could start a mass walkout. Doctor Charles Socarides, associate clinical professor of psychiatry at the Albert Einstein Clinic staunchly opposes the new A.P.A. approach: "The APA has done what all civilizations have trembled to do...tamper with the biologic role between the sexes." Fancy that—and in a letter to *Playboy* in June of 1970, Dr Socarides says, "Five hundred million years of evolution have established the male/female standard as *the* functionally healthy pattern of human sexual fulfillment."

Just a minute here, Doctor—the human species is not more than one million years old according to the earliest human remains so far discovered. Other species have had a longer run. Three hundred million years have established a big mouth that can bite off almost anything and a gut that can digest it, as a functionally healthy pattern for sharks. About 130 million years established large size as functionally healthy for dinosaurs. What may be functionally healthy at one time is not necessarily so under altered conditions, as the bones of discontinued models bear silent witness. But sharks, dinosaurs, and psychiatrists don't want to change.

The sexual revolution is now moving into the electronic stage. Recent experiments in electric brain stimulation indicate that sexual excitement and orgasm can be produced at push-button control or push-button *choice,* depending on who is pushing the buttons. None of these bits of technology are in the future; the knowledge, and most of the hardware, exist today.

For example, there already exists a device that can be used in conjunction with bio-feedback and electric brain stimulation. I quote from an article by Patrick Carr, entitled "The Sonic Dildo: At Last, the No-Contact Orgasm," about how a man named How Wachspress of San Francisco has developed an audio machine that puts sound into the human body through the skin: "He begins to play with the controls of his synthesizer, programming a series of sonic patterns for sensual effect, and this *feeling* begins to spread down from my stomach toward my crotch, most certainly turning me on and relaxing me at the same time. My instant desire is for the same, only louder. Lovely sensations spread over my hips, crotch, stomach, and spine, and I am beginning to sense surprisingly precise nuances of tone and pattern as How performs 'frequency sweeps,' a sharp attack with a long decay, a long rise with a sharp decay…oh, *yes*… 'Very Indian, huh?' says How. 'Y'know, I'm certain that ragas would be great for the body…' Afterward, disconnected from the unit, I experienced a wonderful body-buzzing calm."

In terms of human sexuality what could it mean? Apparently there is no limit. A partner evoked by sophisticated electric brain stimulation could be as real and much more satisfying than the boy or girl next door. The machine can provide you with anything or anybody you want. All the stars in Hollywood living or dead are there for your pleasure. Sated with superstars, you can lay Cleopatra, Helen of Troy, Isis, Madame Pompadour, or Aphrodite. You can get fucked by Pan, Jesus Christ, Apollo or the Devil himself. Anything you like likes you when you press the buttons. Boys, girls, gods, angels, devils. The appropriate sets can also be plugged in. Sex in an Egyptian palace? A Greek glade? A 1910 outhouse? Roman baths? Space capsule? 1920 rumble seat? Pirate ship? Log cabin? Mongol tent? And none of the sweat that goes with log cabins, tents and pirate ships. It's ready built, waiting for you, and you can leave any time you want.

Could real partners compete? Well, maybe. Experiments in autonomic shaping have demonstrated that subjects can learn to control these responses and reproduce them at will once they learn where the neural buttons are located. Just decide what you want, and your local sex adjustment center will match your brain waves and provide you with a suitable mate of whatever sex, real or imaginary, while you wait. It is now possible to provide every man and woman with the best sex tricks he or she can tolerate without blowing a fuse. And any candidate running on that ticket should poll a lot of votes and bring a lot of issues right out into the open.

"I promise you that I will disband the Army and the Navy and channel the entire defense budget into setting up sexual adjustment centers throughout the United States. And I promise you further that the psychic energy generated in these centers will turn any and all prospective enemies into friends, into *intimate* friends, as other nations follow our shining example."

"Control buttons to the People."

Allen Ginsberg

Sweet Boy, Gimme Yr Ass

lemme kiss your face, lick your neck
touch your lips, tongue tickle tongue end
nose to nose, quiet questions
ever slept with a man before?
hand stroking your back slowly down to the cheeks' moist hair soft asshole
eyes to eyes blur, a tear strained from seeing—

Come on boy, fingers thru my hair
Pull my beard, kiss my eyelids, tongue my ear, lips light on my forehead
—met you in the street you carried my package—
Put your hand down to my legs,
touch if it's there, the prick shaft delicate
hot in your rounded palm, soft thumb on cockhead—

Come on come on kiss my full lipped, wet tongue, eyes open—
animal in the zoo looking out of skull cage—you
smile, I'm here so are you, hand tracing your abdomen
from nipple down rib cage smooth skinn'd past belly veins, along muscle
    to your silk-shiny groin
across your long prick down your right thigh
up the smooth road muscle wall to titty again—
Come on go down on me your throat
swallowing my shaft to the base tongue
cock solid suck—
I'll do the same your stiff prick's soft skin, lick your ass—

Come on Come on, open up, legs apart here this pillow

under your buttock
Come on take it here's vaseline the hard on here's
your old ass lying easy up in the air—here's
a hot prick at yr soft-mouthed asshole—just relax and let it in—
Yeah just relax hey Carlos lemme in, I love you, yeah how come
you came here anyway except this kiss this hug this mouth these
    two eyes looking up, this hard slow thrust this
      softness this relaxed sweet sigh?

3 January 1974, to C. R.

Jane Bowles

Going to Massachusetts

[The brilliant and witty Jane Bowles had an incomparable literary voice that is still underappreciated except by other writers. Although mostly lesbian, she married the mostly gay Paul Bowles in 1937. They settled in Tangier in 1948, where they became the center of expatriate literary life, hosting friends like Truman Capote, Tennessee Williams, and Gore Vidal. When the far less glamorous Ginsberg called, he introduced himself as "Allen Ginsberg, the bop poet" and asked Jane if she believed in God. "Well, if I do I'm certainly not discussing it on the telephone," she said before hanging up on him. Although friends with both Paul and Jane Bowles, Burroughs grew especially fond of Jane, and recalled, "She was very, very funny, and she had a sort of chic quality that everyone commented on…she has this very admiring set of [followers] whose eyes would get all misty when they said, 'Oh, Janie!' " Her story "Going to Massachusetts" dates from 1966 and is a fragment of a larger, unfinished work.—ed.]

Bozoe rubbed away some tears with a closed fist.

"Come along, Bozoe," said Janet. "You're not going to the North Pole."

Bozoe tugged at the woolly fur, and pulled a little of it out.

"Leave your coat alone," said Janet.

"I don't remember why I'm going to Massachusetts," Bozoe moaned. "I knew it would be like this, once I got to the station."

"If you don't want to go to Massachusetts," said Janet, "then come on back to the apartment. We'll stop at Fanny's on the way. I want to buy those tumblers made out of knobby glass. I want brown ones."

Bozoe started to cry in earnest. This caused Janet considerable embarrassment. She was conscious of herself as a public figure because the fact that she owned and ran a garage had given her a good deal of publicity not only in East Clinton but in the neighboring counties. This scene, she said to herself, makes us look like two Italians saying goodbye. Everybody'll think we're two Italians. She did not feel true sympathy for Bozoe. Her sense of responsibility was overdeveloped, but she was totally lacking in real tenderness.

"There's no reason for you to cry over a set of whiskey tumblers," said Janet, "I told you ten days ago that I was going to buy them."

"Passengers boarding Bus Number Twenty-seven, northbound...."

"I'm not crying about whiskey tumblers." Bozoe managed with difficulty to get the words out. "I'm crying about Massachusetts. I can't remember my reasons."

"Rockport, Rayville, Muriel...."

"Why don't you listen to the loudspeaker, Bozoe? It's giving you information. If you paid attention to what's going on around you you'd be a lot better off. You concentrate too much on your own private affairs. Try more to be a part of the world."

• • •

"... The truth is that I am only twenty-five miles away from the apartment, as you have probably guessed. In fact, you could not help but guess it, since you are perfectly familiar with Larry's Bar and Grill. I could not go to Massachusetts. I cried the whole way up to Muriel and it was as if someone else were getting off the bus, not myself. But someone who was in a desperate hurry to reach the next stop. I was in mortal terror that the bus would not stop at Muriel but continue on to some further destination where I would not know any familiar face. My terror was so great that I actually stopped crying. I kept from crying all the way. This is a lie. Not an actual lie because I never lie as you know. Small solace to either one of us, isn't it? I am sure that you would prefer me to lie, rather than be so intent on explaining my dilemma to you night and day. I am convinced that you would prefer me to lie. It would give you more time for the garage."

"So?" queried Sis McEvoy, an unkind note in her voice. To Janet she did not sound noticeably unkind, since Sis McEvoy was habitually sharp-sounding, and like her had very little sympathy for other human beings. She was sure that Sis McEvoy was bad, and she was determined to save her. She was going to save her quietly without letting Sis suspect her determination. Janet did everything secretly; in fact, secrecy was the essence of her nature, and from it she derived her pleasure and her sense of being an important member of society.

"What's it all about?" Sis asked irritably. "Why doesn't she raise kids or else go to a psychologist or a psychoanalyst or whatever? My ovaries are crooked or I'd raise kids myself. That's what God's after, isn't it? Space ships or no space ships. What's the problem anyway? How are her ovaries and the rest of the mess?"

Janet smiled mysteriously. "Bozoe has never wanted a child," she said. "She told me she was too scared."

"Don't you despise cowards?" said Sis. "Jesus Christ, they turn my stomach."

Janet frowned. "Bozoe says she despises cowards, too. She worries herself sick about it. She's got it all linked up together with Heaven and Hell. She thinks so much about Heaven and Hell that she's useless. I've told her for years to occupy herself. I've told her that God would like her better if she was occupied. But she says God isn't interested. That's a kind of slam at me, I suppose. It doesn't bother me, but it makes me a little sore when she tries to convince me that I wouldn't be interested in the garage unless she talked to me day and night about her troubles. As if I was interested in the garage just out of spite. I'm a normal woman and I'm interested in my work, like all women are in modern times. I'm a lit-tle stockier than most, I guess, and not fussy or feminine. That's because my father was my ideal and my mother was an alcoholic. I'm stocky and I don't like pretty dresses and I'm interested in my work. My work is like God to me. I don't mean I put it above Him, but the next thing to Him. I have a feeling that he approves of my working. That he approves

—

145

of my working in a garage. Maybe that's cheeky of me, but I can't help it. I've made a name for myself in the garage and I'm decent. I'm normal." She paused for a moment to fill the two whiskey tumblers.

"Do you like my whiskey tumblers?" She was being unusually spry and talkative. "I don't usually have much time to buy stuff. But I had to, of course. Bozoe never bought anything in her life. She's what you'd call a dead weight. She's getting fatter, too, all the time."

"They're good tumblers," said Sis McEvoy. "They hold a lot of whiskey."

Janet flushed slightly at the compliment. She attributed the unaccustomed excitement she felt to her freedom from the presence of Bozoe Flanner.

"Bozoe was very thin when I first knew her," she told Sis. "And she didn't show any signs that she was going to sit night and day making up problems and worrying about God and asking me questions. There wasn't any of that in the beginning. Mainly she was meek, I guess, and she had soft-looking eyes, like a doe or a calf. Maybe she had the problems the whole time and was just planning to spring them on me later. I don't know. I never thought she was going to get so tied up in knots, or so fat either. Naturally if she were heavy and happy too it would be better."

"I have no flesh on my bones at all," said Sis McEvoy, as if she had not even heard the rest of the conversation. "The whole family's thin, and every last one of us has a rotten lousy temper inherited from both sides. My father and my sister had rotten tempers."

"I don't mind if you have a temper display in my apartment," said Janet. "Go to it. I believe in people expressing themselves. If you've inherited a temper there isn't much you can do about it except express it. I think it's much better for you to break this crockery pumpkin, for instance, than to hold your temper in and become unnatural. For instance, I could buy another pumpkin and you'd feel relieved. I'd gather that, at any rate. I don't know much about people, really. I never dabbled in people. They were never my specialty. But surely if you've inherited a temper from both sides it would seem to me that you would have to

—

express it. It isn't your fault, is it, after all?" Janet seemed determined to show admiration for Sis McEvoy.

"I'm having fun," she continued unexpectedly. "It's a long time since I've had any fun. I've been too busy getting the garage into shape. Then there's Bozoe trouble. I've kept to the routine. Late Sunday breakfast with popovers and homemade jam. She eats maybe six of them, but with the same solemn expression on her face. I'm husky but a small eater. We have record players and television. But nothing takes her mind off herself. There's no point in my getting any more machines. I've got the cash and the good will, but there's absolutely no point."

"You seem to be very well set up," said Sis McEvoy, narrowing her eyes. "Here's to you." She tipped her glass and drained it.

Janet filled Sister's glass at once. "I'm having a whale of a good time," she said. "I hope you are. Of course I don't want to butt into your business. Bozoe always thought I pored over my account books for such a long time on purpose. She thought I was purposely trying to get away from her. What do you think, Sis McEvoy?" She asked this almost in a playful tone that bordered on a yet unexpected flirtatiousness.

"I'm not interested in women's arguments with each other," said Sis at once. "I'm interested in women's arguments with men. What else is there? The rest doesn't amount to a row of monkeys."

"Oh, I agree," Janet said, as if she were delighted by this statement which might supply her with the stimulus she was after. "I agree one thousand percent. Remember I spend more time in the garage with the men than I do with Bozoe Flanner."

"I'm not actually living with my husband because of my temper," said Sis. "I don't like long-standing relationships. They disagree with me. I get the blues. I don't want anyone staying in my life for a long time. It gives me the creeps. Men are crazy about me. I like the cocktails and the compliments. Then after a while they turn my stomach."

"You're a very interesting woman," Janet Murphy announced, throwing caution to the winds and finding it pleasant.

—

"I know I'm interesting," said Sis. "But I'm not so sure life is interesting."

"Are you interested in money?" Janet asked her. "I don't mean money for the sake of money, but for buying things."

Sis did not answer, and Janet feared that she had been rude. "I didn't mean to hurt your feelings," she said. "After all, money comes up in everybody's life. Even duchesses have to talk about money. But I won't, any more. Come on. Let's shake." She held out her hand to Sis McEvoy, but Sis allowed it to stay there foolishly, without accepting the warm grip Janet had intended for her.

"I'm really sorry," she went on, "if you think I was trying to be insulting and personal. I honestly was not. The fact is that I have been so busy building up a reputation for the garage that I behave like a savage. I'll never mention money again." In her heart she felt that Sis was somehow pleased that the subject had been brought up, but was not yet ready to admit it. Sis's tedious work at the combination tearoom and soda fountain where they had met could scarcely make her feel secure.

Bozoe doesn't play one single feminine trick, she told herself, and after all, after struggling nearly ten years to build up a successful and unusual business I'm entitled to some returns. I'm in a rut with Bozoe and this Sis is going to get me out of it. (By now she was actually furious with Bozoe.) I'm entitled to some fun. The men working for me have more fun than I have.

"I feel grateful to you, Sis," she said without explaining her remark. "You've done me a service. May I tell you that I admire your frankness, without offending you?"

Sis McEvoy was beginning to wonder if Janet were another nut like Bozoe Flanner. This worried her a little, but she was too drunk by now for clear thinking. She was enjoying the compliments, although it was disturbing that they should be coming from a woman. She was very proud of never having been depraved or abnormal, and pleased to be merely mean and discontented to the extent of not having been able to

—

stay with any man for longer than the three months she had spent with her husband.

"I'll read you more of Bozoe's letter," Janet suggested.

"I can't wait," said Sis. "I can't wait to hear a lunatic's mind at work first-hand. Her letter's so cheerful and elevating. And so constructive. Go to it. But fill my glass first so I can concentrate. I'd hate to miss a word. It would kill me."

Janet realized it was unkind of her to be reading a friend's letter to someone who so obviously had only contempt for it. But she felt no loyalty—only eagerness to make Sis see how hard her life had been. She felt that in this way the bond between them might be strengthened.

"Well, here it comes," she said. "Stop me when you can't stand it any more. *I know that you expected me to come back. You did not feel I had the courage to carry out my scheme. I still expect to work it out. But not yet. I am more than ever convinced that my salvation lies in solitude, and coming back to the garage before I have even reached Massachusetts would be a major defeat for me, as I'm sure you must realize, even though you pretend not to know what I'm talking about most of the time. I am convinced that you do know what I'm talking about and if you pretend ignorance of my dilemma so you can increase efficiency at the garage you are going to defeat yourself. I can't actually save you, but I can point little things out to you constantly. I refer to your soul, nationally, and not to any success you've had or to your determination. In any case it came to me on the bus that it was not time for me to leave you, and that although going to Massachusetts required more courage and strength than I seemed able to muster, I was at the same time being very selfish in going. Selfish because I was thinking in terms of my salvation and not yours. I'm glad I thought of this. It is why I stopped crying and got off the bus. Naturally you would disapprove, because I had paid for my ticket which is now wasted, if for no other reason. That's the kind of thing you would like me to think about, isn't it? It makes you feel that I'm more human. I have never admired being human, I must say. I want to be like God. But I haven't begun yet. First I have to go to Massachusetts and be* alone. But I got off the bus. And I've wasted the fare. I can hear you stressing that above all else, as I say. But I want you to understand that it was not cowardice alone that stopped me from going to Massachusetts. I don't feel that I can allow you to sink into the mire of contentment and happy ambitious enterprise. It is my duty to prevent you from it as much as I do for myself. It is not fair of me to go away until you completely understand how I feel about God and my destiny. Surely we have been brought together for some purpose, even if that purpose ends by our being separate again. But not until the time is ripe. Naturally, the psychiatrists would at once declare that I was laboring under a compulsion. I am violently against psychiatry, and, in fact, against happiness. Though of course I love it. I love happiness, I mean. Of course you would not believe this. Naturally darling I love you, and I'm afraid that if you don't start suffering soon God will take some terrible vengeance. It is better for you to offer yourself. Don't accept social or financial security as your final aim. Or fame is the garage. Fame is unworthy of you; that is, the desire for it. Janet, my beloved, I do not expect you to be gloomy or fanatical as I am. I do not believe that God intended you for quite as harrowing a destiny as He did for me. I don't mean this as an insult. I believe you should actually thank your stars. I would really like to be fulfilling humble daily chores myself and listening to a concert at night or television or playing a card game. But I can find no rest, and I don't think you should either. At least not until you have fully understood my dilemma on earth. That means that you must no longer turn a deaf ear to me and pretend that your preoccupation with the garage is in a sense a holier absorption than trying to understand and fully realize the importance and meaning of my dilemma. I think that you hear more than you admit, too. There is a stubborn streak in your nature working against you, most likely unknown to yourself. An insistence on being shallow rather than profound. I repeat: I do not expect you to be as profound as I am. But to insist on exploiting the most shallow side of one's nature, out of stubbornness and merely because it is more pleasant to be shallow, is certainly a sin. Sis McEvoy will help you to express the shallow side of your nature, by the way. Like a toboggan slide."

Janet stopped abruptly, appalled at having read this last part aloud. She had not expected Bozoe to mention Sis at all. "Gee," she said. "Gosh! She's messing everything up together, I'm awfully sorry."

Sis McEvoy stood up and walked unsteadily to the television set. Some of her drink slopped onto the rug as she went. She faced Janet with fierce eyes. "There's nobody in the world who can talk to me like that, and there's not going to be. Never!" She was leaning on the set and steadying herself against it with both hands. "I'll keep on building double-decker sandwiches all my life first. It's five flights to the top of the building where I live. It's an insurance building, life insurance, and I'm the only woman who lives there. I have boy friends come when they want to. I don't have to worry, either. I'm crooked so I don't have to bother with abortions or any other kind of mess. The hell with television anyway."

She likes the set, Janet said to herself. She felt more secure. "Bozoe and I don't have the same opinions at all," she said. "We don't agree on anything."

"Who cares? You live in the same apartment, don't you? You've lived in the same apartment for ten years. Isn't that all anybody's got to know?" She rapped with her fist on the wood panelling of the television set. "Whose is it, anyhow?" She was growing increasingly aggressive.

"It's mine," Janet said. "It's my television set." She spoke loud so that Sis would be sure to catch her words.

"What the hell do I care?" cried Sis. "I live on top of a life-insurance building and I work in a combination soda-fountain lunch-room. Now read me the rest of the letter."

"I don't think you really want to hear any more of Bozoe's non-sense," Janet said smoothly. "She's spoiling our evening together. There's no reason for us to put up with it all. Why should we? Why don't I make something to eat? Not a sandwich. You must be sick of sandwiches."

"What I eat is my own business," Sis snapped.

"Naturally," said Janet. "I thought you might like something hot like bacon and eggs. Nice crisp bacon and eggs." She hoped to persuade her so that she might forget about the letter.

—

"I don't like food," said Sis. "I don't even like millionaires' food, so don't waste your time."

"I'm a small eater myself." She had to put off reading Bozoe's letter until Sis had forgotten about it. "My work at the garage requires some sustenance, of course. But it's brainwork now more than manual labor. Being a manager's hard on the brain."

Sis looked at Janet and said: "Your brain doesn't impress me. Or that garage. I like newspaper men. Men who are champions. Like champion boxers. I've known lots of champions. They take to me. Champions all fall for me, but I'd never want any of them to find out that I knew someone like your Bozoe. They'd lose their respect."

"I wouldn't introduce Bozoe to a boxer, either, or anybody else who was interested in sports. I know they'd be bored. I know." She waited. "You're very nice. Very intelligent. You *know* people. That's an asset."

"Stay with Bozoe and her television set," Sis growled.

"It's not her television set. It's mine, Sis. Why don't you sit down? Sit on the couch over there."

"The apartment belongs to both of you, and so does the set. I know what kind of a couple you are. The whole world knows it. I could put you in jail if I wanted to. I could put you and Bozoe both in jail."

In spite of these words she stumbled over to the couch and sat down. "Whiskey," she demanded. "The world loves drunks but it despises perverts. Athletes and boxers drink when they're not in training. All the time."

Janet went over to her and served her a glass of whiskey with very little ice. Let's hope she'll pass out, she said to herself. She couldn't see Sis managing the steps up to her room in the insurance building, and in any case she didn't want her to leave. She's such a relief after Bozoe, she thought. Alive and full of fighting spirit. She's much more my type, coming down to facts. She thought it unwise to go near Sis, and was careful to pour the fresh drink quickly and return to her own seat. She would have preferred to sit next to Sis, in spite of her mention of jail, but

—

152

she did not relish being punched or smacked in the face. It's all Bozoe's fault, she said to herself. That's what she gets for thinking she's God. Her holy words can fill a happy peaceful room with poison from twenty-five miles away.

"I love my country," said Sis, for no apparent reason. "I love it to death!"

"Sure you do, Hon," said Janet. "I could murder Bozoe for upsetting you with her loony talk. You were so peaceful until she came in."

"Read that letter," said Sister. After a moment she repeated, as if from a distance: "Read the letter."

Janet was perplexed. Obviously food was not going to distract Sis, and she had nothing left to suggest, in any case, but some Gorton's Codfish made into cakes, and she did not dare to offer her these.

What a rumpus that would raise, she said to herself. And if I suggest turning on the television she'll raise the roof. Stay off television and codfish cakes until she's normal again. Working at a lunch counter is no joke.

There was nothing she could do but do as Sis told her and hope that she might fall asleep while she was reading her the letter. "Damn Bozoe anyway," she muttered audibly.

"Don't put on any acts," said Sis, clearly awake. "I hate liars and I always smell an act. Even though I didn't go to college. I have no respect for college."

"I didn't go to college," Janet began, hoping Sis might be led on to a new discussion. "I went to commercial school."

"Shut up, God damn you! Nobody ever tried to make a commercial school sound like an interesting topic except you. Nobody! You're out of your mind. Read the letter."

"Just a second," said Janet, knowing there was no hope for her. "Let me put my glasses on and find my place. Doing accounts at the garage year in and year out has ruined my eyes. My eyes used to be perfect." She added this weakly, without hope of arousing either sympathy or interest.

—

Sis did not deign to answer.

"Well, here it is again," she began apologetically. "Here it is in all its glory." She poured a neat drink to give herself courage. *"As I believe I just wrote you, I have been down to the bar and brought a drink back with me. (One more defeat for me, a defeat which is of course a daily occurrence, and I daresay I should not bother to mention in this letter.) In any case I could certainly not face being without one after the strain of actually boarding the bus, even if I did get off without having the courage to stick on it until I got where I was going. However, please keep in mind the second reason I had for stopping short of my destination. Please read it over carefully so that you will not have only contempt for me. The part about the responsibility I feel toward you. The room here over Larry's Bar and Grill is dismal. It is one of several rented out by Larry's sister whom we met a year ago when we stopped here for a meal. You remember. It was the day we took Stretch for a ride and let him out of the car to run in the woods, that scanty patch of woods you found just as the sun was setting, and you kept picking up branches that were stuck together with wet leaves and dirt...."*

Harold Norse

Horns

For Lawrence Ferlinghetti

On the Chinatown corner of Broadway and Grant
an old man in skins and furs
with occult ornaments and symbols
is shaking a large cowbell.
In his other hand a brown lacquered staff ends in a two-pronged fork.

Around his belly a pair of bull's horns,
his fur-crowned head slowly swaying
from left to right
as in some ancient shamanistic ritual,
ceremonies out of the past.

Near him a Chinese boy locked in a deep throaty kiss with a dumpy
blonde.

A white boy shoves the mouth end of a long horn
in rhythmic movements
up the Chinese boy's ass,
then blows the horn and inserts it again.

When the kiss breaks up the Chinese boy drunkenly thanks the white
boy
who disappears with the still-dazed girl. The white boy's hand
grazes in quick succession four big erections

—

as a group of tall youths pushes drunkenly by in the tight-wedged mass.

. . .

I'm pressed like a piece of paper in the mob,
like a page in a book.
Bodies pass through me and I through them.
Everyone wants to burst out of their clothes,
press flesh into flesh.

The streets are lined with blow-ups of naked women in topless
                                                bottomless shows.

The barkers scream: COME IN AND GET DRUNK AND HORNY!

and the madness of crowds
is the madness of unreleased energy.

. . .

I go home with images of bodies.
I go home with the imprint of smiles.

I go home with the dry taste
and feel of untouched skin.

I go home with the flank of the cavalry horse
and the horseman's boot grazing my cheek.

I go home with the stench of the cossack's horse
lifting its tail, letting go on the crowd.

—

I go home with the guns from the rooftops,
the deadly control of the State.

I go home sloshing towards others,
love flooding the curbs in waves.

I go home with the iron of separation
embedded in my life.

San Francisco, 2.1.75

William Burroughs

from The Place of Dead Roads

Sunset through black clouds…red glow on naked bodies. Kim carefully wraps his revolver in a towel and places it under some weeds at the water's edge. He puts his foot in the water and gasps. At this moment Tom streaks by him, floating above the ground in a series of still pictures, the muscles of his thigh and buttock outlined like an anatomical drawing as he runs straight into the water, silver drops fanning out from his legs.

Kim follows, holding his breath, then swimming rapidly up and down. He treads water, breathing in gasps as the sky darkens and the water stretches black and sinister as if some monster might rise from its depths… In knee-deep water, soaping themselves and looking at each other serene as dogs, their genitals crinkled from the icy water…drying themselves on a sandbank, wiping the sand from his feet…following Tom's lean red buttocks back to the wagon. He stations Kim at the end of the wagon…. "Stand right there," facing the setting sun. Tom pulls a black cloth out of the air with a flourish, bowing to an audience. He stands behind the camera with the black cloth over his head…. "Look at the camera…hands at your sides."

Kim could feel the phantom touch of the lens on his body, light as a breath of wind. Tom is standing naked behind the camera.

"I want to bottle you, mate," Tom says. Kim has never heard this expression but he immediately understands it. And he glimpses a hidden meaning, a forgotten language, sniggering half-heard words of tenderness and doom from lips spotted with decay that send the blood racing to his crotch and singing in his ears as his penis stretches, sways, and stiffens and naked lust surfaces in his face from the dark depths of human origins.

Tom is getting hard too. The shaft is pink and smooth, no veins protruding. Now fully erect, the tip almost touches the delineated muscles of his lean red-brown stomach. At the crown of his cock, on top, is an indentation, as if the creator had left his thumbprint there in damp clay. Held in a film medium, like soft glass, they are both motionless except for the throbbing of tumescent flesh...

"Hold it!"... CLICK... For six seconds the sun seems to stand still in the sky.

Paul Bowles

Pages from Cold Point

[Critic Leslie Fiedler dubbed Paul Bowles "the pornographer of terror." This alone would have attracted William Burroughs, who was inspired to move to Tangier after reading Bowles. Because his friendship with Burroughs and the others dates from the mid-1950s—too late in their careers for much stylistic influence—Bowles is not truly one of the Beats. But their shared interests in drugs, magic, and local boys made for engaging conversation and some cross-fertilization in later years. Much of Bowles's work has homoerotic content, but he was famously silent about his private life. Burroughs joked that his auto-biography, *Without Stopping*, should be retitled *Without Telling*. Incidentally, the last meeting of Bowles, Burroughs, and Ginsberg (also John Giorno) was captured in Rachel Baichwal's documentary on Bowles, *Let It Come Down* (1999). Bowles wrote "Pages from Cold Point" en route to Tangier with his wife, Jane, in 1947.—ed.]

Our civilization is doomed to a short life: its component parts are too heterogeneous. I personally am content to see everything in the process of decay. The bigger the bombs, the quicker it will be done. Life is visually too hideous for one to make the attempt to preserve it. Let it go. Perhaps some day another form of life will come along. Either way, it is of no consequence. At the same time, I am still a part of life, and I am bound by this to protect myself to whatever extent I am able. And so I am here. Here in the Islands vegetation still has the upper hand, and man has to fight even to make his presence seen at all. It is beautiful here, the trade winds blow all year, and I suspect that bombs are extremely unlikely to be wasted on this unfrequented side of the island, if indeed on any part of it.

I was loath to give up the house after Hope's death. But it was the obvious move to make. My university career always having been an utter farce (since I believe no reason inducing a man to "teach" can possibly be a valid one), I was elated by the idea of resigning, and as soon as her affairs had been settled and the money properly invested, I lost no time in doing so.

I think that week was the first time since childhood that I had managed to recapture the feeling of there being a content in existence. I went from one pleasant house to the next, making my adieux to the English quacks, the Philosophy fakirs, and so on—even to those colleagues with whom I was merely on speaking terms. I watched the envy on their faces when I announced my departure by Pan American on Saturday morning; and the greatest pleasure I felt in all this was in being able to answer, "Nothing," when I was asked, as invariably I was, what I intended to do.

When I was a boy people used to refer to Charles as "Big Brother C.," although he is only a scant year older than I. To me now he is merely "Fat Brother C.," a successful lawyer. His thick, red face and hands, his backslapping joviality, and his fathomless hypocritical prudery, these are the qualities which make him truly repulsive to me. There is also the fact that he once looked not unlike the way Racky does now. And after all, he still is my big brother, and disapproves openly of everything I do. The loathing that I feel for him is so strong that for years I have not been able to swallow a morsel of food or a drop of liquid in his presence without making a prodigious effort. No one knows this but me—certainly not Charles, who would be the last one I would tell about it. He came up on the late train two nights before I left. He got quickly to the point—as soon as he was settled with a highball.

"So you're off for the wilds," he said, sitting forward in his chair like a salesman.

"If you can call it the wilds," I replied. "Certainly it's not wild like Mitichi." (He has a lodge in northern Quebec.) "I consider it really civilized."

He drank and smacked his lips together stiffly, bringing the glass down hard on his knee.

"And Racky. You're taking him along?"

"Of course."

"Out of school. Away. So he'll see nobody but you. You think that's good."

I looked at him. "I do," I said.

"By God, if I could stop you legally, I would!" he cried, jumping up and putting his glass on the mantel. I was trembling inwardly with excitement, but I merely sat and watched him. He went on. "You're not fit to have custody of the kid!" he shouted. He shot a stern glance at me over his spectacles.

"You think not?" I said gently.

Again he looked at me sharply. "D'ye think I've forgotten?"

I was understandably eager to get him out of the house as soon as I could. As I piled and sorted letters and magazines on the desk, I said: "Is that all you came to tell me? I have a good deal to do tomorrow and I must get some sleep. I probably shan't see you at breakfast. Agnes'll see that you eat in time to make the early train."

All he said was: "God! Wake up! Get wise to yourself! You're not fooling anybody, you know."

That kind of talk is typical of Charles. His mind is slow and obtuse; he constantly imagines that everyone he meets is playing some private game of deception with him. He is so utterly incapable of following the functioning of even a moderately evolved intellect that he finds the will to secretiveness and duplicity everywhere.

"I haven't time to listen to that sort of nonsense," I said, preparing to leave the room.

But he shouted, "You don't want to listen! No! Of course not! You just want to do what you want to do. You just want to go on off down there and live as you've a mind to, and to hell with the consequences!" At this point I heard Racky coming downstairs. C. obviously heard nothing and he raved on. "But just remember, I've got your number all right, and if there's any trouble with the boy I'll know who's to blame."

I hurried across the room and opened the door so he could see that Racky was there in the hallway. That stopped his tirade. It was hard to know whether Racky had heard any of it or not. Although he is not a quiet young person, he is the soul of discretion, and it is almost never possible to know any more about what goes on inside his head than he intends one to know.

I was annoyed that C. should have been bellowing at me in my own house. To be sure, he is the only one from whom I would accept such behavior, but then, no father likes to have his son see him take criticism meekly. Racky simply stood there in his bathrobe, his angelic face quite devoid of expression, saying: "Tell Uncle Charley goodnight for me, will you? I forgot."

I said I would, and quickly shut the door. When I thought Racky was back upstairs in his room, I bade Charles good night. I have never been able to get out of his presence fast enough. The effect he has on me dates from an early period in our lives, from days I dislike to recall.

Racky is a wonderful boy. After we arrived, when we found it impossible to secure a proper house near any town where he might have the company of English boys and girls his own age, he showed no signs of chagrin, although he must have been disappointed. Instead, as we went out of the renting office into the glare of the street, he grinned and said: "Well, I guess we'll have to get bikes, that's all."

The few available houses near what Charles would have called "civilization" turned out to be so ugly and so impossibly confining in atmosphere that we decided immediately on Cold Point, even though it was across the island and quite isolated on its seaside cliff. It was beyond a doubt one of the most desirable properties on the island, and Racky was as enthusiastic about its splendors as I.

"You'll get tired of being alone out there, just with me," I said to him as we walked back to the hotel.

"Aw, I'll get along all right. When do we look for the bikes?"

At his insistence we bought two the next morning. I was sure I should not make much use of mine, but I reflected that an extra bicycle might be convenient to have around the house. It turned out that the servants all had their own bicycles, without which they would not have been able to get to and from the village of Orange Walk, eight miles down the shore. So for a while I was forced to get astride mine each morning before breakfast and pedal madly along beside Racky for a half hour. We would ride through the cool early air, under the towering silk-cotton trees near the house, and out to the great curve in the shoreline where the waving palms bend landward in the stiff breeze that always blows there. Then we would make a wide turn and race back to the house, loudly discussing the degrees of our desires for various items of breakfast we knew were awaiting us there on the terrace. Back home we would eat in the wind, looking out over the Caribbean, and talk about the news in yesterday's local paper, brought to us by Isiah each morning from Orange Walk. Then Racky would disappear for the whole morning on his bicycle, riding furiously along the road in one direction or the other until he had discovered an unfamiliar strip of sand along the shore that he could consider a new beach. At lunch he would describe it in detail to me, along with a recounting of all the physical hazards involved in hiding the bicycle in among the trees, so that natives passing along the road on foot would not spot it, or in climbing down unscalable cliffs that turned out to be much higher than they had appeared at first sight, or in measuring the depth of the water preparatory to diving from the rocks, or in judging the efficacy of the reef in barring sharks and barracuda. There is never an element of bragadoccio in Racky's relating of his exploits—only the joyous excitement he derives from telling how he satisfies his inexhaustible curiosity. And his mind shows its alertness in all directions at once. I do not mean to say that I expect him to be an "intellectual." That is no affair of mine, nor do I have any particular interest in whether he turns out to be a thinking man or not. I know he

—

will always have a certain boldness of manner and a great purity of spirit in judging values. The former will prevent his becoming what I call a "victim": he never will be brutalized by realities. And his unerring sense of balance in ethical considerations will shield him from the paralyzing effects of present-day materialism.

For a boy of sixteen Racky has an extraordinary innocence of vision. I do not say this as a doting father, although God knows I can never even think of the boy without that familiar overwhelming sensation of delight and gratitude for being vouchsafed the privilege of sharing my life with him. What he takes so completely as a matter of course, our daily life here together, is a source of never-ending wonder to me; and I reflect upon it a good part of each day, just sitting here being conscious of my great good fortune in having him all to myself, beyond the reach of prying eyes and malicious tongues. (I suppose I am really thinking of C. when I write that.) And I believe that a part of the charm of sharing Racky's life with him consists precisely in his taking it all so utterly for granted. I have never asked him whether he likes being here—it is so patent that he does, very much. I think if he were to turn to me one day and tell me how happy he is here, that somehow, perhaps, the spell might be broken. Yet if he were to be thoughtless and inconsiderate, or even unkind to me, I feel that I should be able only to love him the more for it.

I have reread that last sentence. What does it mean? And why should I even imagine it should mean anything more than it says?

Still, much as I may try, I can never believe in the gratuitous, isolated fact. What I must mean is that I feel that Racky already has been in some way inconsiderate. But in what way? Surely I cannot resent his bicycle treks; I cannot expect him to want to stay and sit talking with me all day. And I never worry about his being in danger; I know he is more capable than most adults of taking care of himself, and that he is no more likely than any native to come to harm crawling over the cliffs or swimming in the bays. At the same time there is no doubt in my mind that something about our existence annoys me. I must resent some detail in the pattern, whatever that pattern may be. Perhaps it is just his youth, and I am envious of the lithe body, the smooth skin, the animal energy and grace.

For a long time this morning I sat looking out to sea, trying to solve that small puzzle. Two white herons came and perched on a dead stump east of the garden. They stayed a long time there without stirring. I would turn my head away and accustom my eyes to the bright sea-horizon, then I would look suddenly at them to see if they had shifted position, but they would always be in the same attitude. I tried to imagine the black stump without them—a pure vegetable landscape—but it was impossible. All the while I was slowly forcing myself to accept a ridiculous explanation of my annoyance with Racky. It had made itself manifest to me only yesterday, when instead of appearing for lunch, he sent a young colored boy from Orange Walk to say that he would be lunching in the village. I could not help noticing that the boy was riding Racky's bicycle. I had been waiting lunch a good half hour for him, and I had Gloria serve immediately as the boy rode off, back to the village. I was curious to know in what sort of place and with whom Racky could be eating, since Orange Walk, as far as I know, is inhabited exclusively by Negroes, and I was sure Gloria would be able to shed some light on the matter, but I could scarcely ask her. However, as she brought on the dessert, I said: "Who was that boy that brought the message from Mister Racky?"

She shrugged her shoulders. "A young lad of Orange Walk. He's named Wilmot."

When Racky returned at dusk, flushed from his exertion (for he never rides casually), I watched him closely. His behavior struck my already suspicious eye as being one of false heartiness and a rather forced good humor. He went to his room early and read for quite a while before turning off his light. I took a long walk in the almost day-bright moonlight, listening to the songs of the night insects in the trees. And I sat for a while in the dark on the stone railing of the bridge across Black River. (It is really only a brook that rushes down over the rocks from the mountain a few miles inland, to the beach near the house.) In the night it always sounds louder and more important than it does in the daytime. The music of the water over the stones relaxed my nerves, although why I had need of such a thing I find it difficult to understand, unless I was really upset by Racky's not having come home for lunch. But if that were true it would be absurd, and moreover, dangerous—just the sort of thing the parent of an adolescent has to be beware of and fight against, unless he is indifferent to the prospect of losing the trust and affection of his offspring permanently. Racky must stay out whenever he likes, with whom he likes, and for as long as he likes, and I must not think twice about it, much less mention it to him, or in any way give the impression of prying. Lack of confidence on the part of a parent is the one unforgivable sin.

Although we still take our morning dip together on arising, it is three weeks since we have been for the early spin. One morning I found that Racky had jumped onto his bicycle in his wet trunks while I was still swimming, and gone by himself, and since then there has been an unspoken agreement between us that such is to be the procedure; he will go alone. Perhaps I held him back; he likes to ride so fast.

Young Peter, the smiling gardener from Saint Ives Cove, is Racky's special friend. It is amusing to see them together among the bushes, crouched over an ant-hill or rushing about trying to catch a lizard, almost of an age the two, yet so disparate—Racky with his tan skin looking almost white in contrast to the glistening black of the other. Today I know I shall be alone for lunch, since it is Peter's day off. On such days they usually go together on their bicycles into Saint Ives Cove, where Peter keeps a small rowboat. They fish along the coast there, but they have never returned with anything so far.

Meanwhile I am here alone, sitting on the rocks in the sun, from time to time climbing down to cool myself in the water, always conscious of the house behind me under the high palms, like a large glass boat filled with orchids and lilies. The servants are clean and quiet, and the work seems to be accomplished almost automatically. The good, black servants are another blessing of the islands; the British, born here in this paradise, have no conception of how fortunate they are. In fact, they do nothing but complain. One must have lived in the United States to appreciate the wonder of this place. Still, even here ideas are changing each day. Soon the people will decide that they want their land to be a part of today's monstrous world, and once that happens, it will be all over. As soon as you have that desire, you are infected with the deadly virus, and you begin to show the symptoms of the disease. You live in terms of time and money, and you think in terms of society and progress. Then all that is left for you is to kill the other people who think the same way, along with a good many of those who do not, since that is the final manifestation of the malady. Here for the moment at any rate, one has a feeling of staticity— existence ceases to be like those last few seconds in the hour-glass when what is left of the sand suddenly begins to rush through to the bottom all at once. For the moment, it seems suspended. And if it seems, it is. Each wave at my feet, each bird-call in the forest at my back, does *not* carry me one step nearer the final disaster. The disaster is certain, but it will suddenly have happened, that is all. Until then, time stays still.

I am upset by a letter in this morning's mail: The Royal Bank of Canada requests that I call in person at its central office to sign the deposit slips and other papers for a sum that was cabled from the bank in Boston. Since the central office is on the other side of the island, fifty miles away, I shall have to spend the night over there and return the following day. There is no point in taking Racky along. The sight of "civilization" might awaken a longing for it in him; one never knows. I am sure it would have in me when I was his age. And if that should once start, he would merely be unhappy, since there is nothing for him but to stay here with me, at least for the next two years, when I hope to renew the lease, or, if things in New York pick up, buy the place. I am sending word by

Isiah when he goes home into Orange Walk this evening, to have the McCoigh car call for me at seven-thirty tomorrow morning. It is an enormous old open Packard, and Isiah can save the ride out to work here by piling his bicycle into the back and riding with McCoigh.

The trip across the island was beautiful, and would have been highly enjoyable if my imagination had not played me a strange trick at the very outset. We stopped in Orange Walk for gasoline, and while that was being seen to, I got out and went to the corner store for some cigarettes. Since it was not yet eight o'clock, the store was still closed, and I hurried up the side street to the other little shop which I thought might be open. It was, and I bought my cigarettes. On the way back to the corner I noticed a large black woman leaning with her arms on the gate in front of her tiny house, staring into the street. As I passed by her, she looked straight into my face and said something with the strange accent of the island. It was said in what seemed an unfriendly tone, and ostensibly was directed at me, but I had no notion what it was. I got back into the car and the driver started it. The sound of the words had stayed in my head, however, as a bright shape outlined by darkness is likely to stay in the mind's eye, in such a way that when one shuts one's eyes one can see the exact contour of the shape. The car was already roaring up the hill toward the overland road when I suddenly reheard the very words. And they were: "Keep your boy at home, mahn." I sat perfectly rigid for a moment as the open countryside rushed past. Why should I think she had said that? Immediately I decided that I was giving an arbitrary sense to a phrase I could not have understood even if I had been paying strict attention. And then I wondered why my subconscious should have chosen that sense, since now that I whispered the words over to myself they failed to connect with any anxiety to which my mind might have been disposed. Actually I have never given a thought to Racky's wanderings about Orange Walk. I can find no such preoccupation no matter how I put the question to myself. Then, could she really have said those words?

—

All the way through the mountains I pondered the question, even though it was obviously a waste of energy. And soon I could no longer hear the sounds of her voice in my memory: I had played the record over too many times, and worn it out.

Here in the hotel a gala dance is in progress. The abominable orchestra, comprising two saxophones and one sour violin, is playing directly under my window in the garden, and the serious-looking couples slide about on the waxed concrete floor of the terrace, in the light of strings of paper lanterns. I suppose it is meant to look Japanese.

At this moment I wonder what Racky is doing there in the house with only Peter and Ernest the watchman to keep him company. I wonder if he is asleep. The house, which I am accustomed to think of as smiling and benevolent in its airiness, could just as well be in the most sinister and remote regions of the globe, now that I am here. Sitting here with the absurd orchestra bleating downstairs, I picture it to myself, and it strikes me as terribly vulnerable in its isolation. In my mind's eye I see the moonlit point with its tall palms waving restlessly in the wind, its dark cliffs licked by the waves below. Suddenly, although I struggle against the sensation, I am inexpressibly glad to be away from the house, helpless there, far on its point of land, in the silence of the night. Then I remember that the night is seldom silent. There is the loud sea at the base of the rocks, the droning of the thousands of insects, the occasional cries of the night birds—all the familiar noises that make sleep so sound. And Racky is there surrounded by them as usual, not even hearing them. But I feel profoundly guilty for having left him, unutterably tender and sad at the thought of him, lying there alone in the house with the two Negroes the only human beings within miles. If I keep thinking of Cold Point I shall be more and more nervous.

I am not going to bed yet. They are all screaming with laughter down there, the idiots; I could never sleep anyway. The bar is still open. Fortunately it is on the street side of the hotel. For once I need a few drinks.

Much later, but I feel no better; I may be a little drunk. The dance is over and it is quiet in the garden, but the room is too hot.

As I was falling asleep last night, all dressed, and with the overhead light shining sordidly in my face, I heard the black woman's voice again, more clearly even than I did in the car yesterday. For some reason this morning there is no doubt in my mind that the words I heard are the words she said. I accept that and go on from there. Suppose she did tell me to keep Racky home. It could only mean that she, or someone else in Orange Walk, has had a childish altercation with him; although I must say it is hard to conceive of Racky's entering into any sort of argument or feud with these people. To set my mind at rest (for I do seem to be taking the thing with great seriousness), I am going to stop in the village this afternoon before going home, and try to see the woman. I am extremely curious to know what she could have meant.

I had not been conscious until this evening when I came back to Cold Point how powerful they are, all those physical elements that go to make up its atmosphere: the sea and wind-sounds that isolate the house from the road, the brilliancy of the water, sky and sun, the bright colors and strong odors of the flowers, the feeling of space both outside and within the house. One naturally accepts these things when one is living here. This afternoon when I returned I was conscious of them all over again, of their existence and their strength. All of them together are like a powerful drug; coming back made me feel as though I had been disintoxicated and were returning to the scene of my former indulgences. Now at eleven it is as if I had never been absent an hour. Everything is the same as always, even to the dry palm branch that scrapes against the window screen by my night table. And indeed, it is only thirty-six hours since I was here; but I always expect my absence from a place to bring about irremediable changes.

Strangely enough, now that I think of it, I feel that something *has* changed since I left yesterday morning, and that is the general attitude of the servants—their collective aura, so to speak. I noticed that difference immediately upon arriving back, but was unable to define it. Now I see it clearly. The network of common understanding which slowly spreads itself through a well-run household has been destroyed. Each person is by himself now. No unfriendliness, however, that I can see. They all behave with the utmost courtesy, excepting possibly Peter, who struck me as looking unaccustomedly glum when I encountered him in the kitchen after dinner. I meant to ask Racky if he had noticed it, but I forgot and he went to bed early.

In Orange Walk I made a brief stop on the pretext to McCoigh that I wanted to see the seamstress in the side street. I walked up and back in front of the house where I had seen the woman, but there was no sign of anyone.

As for my absence, Racky seems to have been perfectly content, having spent most of the day swimming off the rocks below the terrace. The insect sounds are at their height now, the breeze is cooler than usual, and I shall take advantage of these favorable conditions to get a good long night's rest.

Today has been one of the most difficult days of my life. I arose early, we had breakfast at the regular time, and Racky went off in the direction of Saint Ives Cove. I lay in the sun on the terrace for a while, listening to the noises of the household's regime. Peter was all over the property, collecting dead leaves and fallen blossoms in a huge basket and carrying them off to the compost heap. He appeared to be in an even fouler humor than last night. When he came near to me at one point on his way to another part of the garden I called to him. He set the basket down and stood looking at me; then he walked across the grass toward me slowly—reluctantly, it seemed to me.

"Peter, is everything all right with you?"

"Yes, sir."

"No trouble at home?"

"Oh, no, sir."

"Good."

"Yes, sir."

He went back to his work. But his face belied his words. Not only did he seem to be in a decidedly unpleasant temper; out here in the sunlight he looked positively ill. However, it was not my concern, if he refused to admit to it.

When the heavy heat of the sun reached the unbearable point for me, I got out of my chair and went down the side of the cliff along the series of steps cut there into the rock. A level platform is below, and a diving board, for the water is deep. At each side, the rocks spread out and the waves break over them, but by the platform the wall of rock is vertical and the water merely hits against it below the springboard. The place is a tiny amphitheatre, quite cut off in sound and sight from the house. There too I like to lie in the sun; when I climb out of the water I often remove my trunks and lie stark naked on the springboard. I regularly make fun of Racky because he is embarrassed to do the same. Occasionally he will do it, but never without being coaxed. I was spread out there without a stitch on, being lulled by the slapping of the water, when an unfamiliar voice very close to me said: "Mister Norton?"

I jumped with nervousness, nearly fell off the springboard, and sat up, reaching at the same time, but in vain, for my trunks, which were lying on the rock practically at the feet of a middle-aged mulatto gentleman. He was in a white duck suit, and wore a high collar with a black tie, and it seemed to me that he was eyeing me with a certain degree of horror.

My next reaction was one of anger at being trespassed upon in this way. I rose and got the trunks, however, donning them calmly and saying nothing more meaningful than: "I didn't hear you coming down the steps."

"Shall we go up?" said my caller. As he led the way, I had a definite premonition that he was here on an unpleasant errand. On the terrace we sat down, and he offered me an American cigarette which I did not accept.

"This is a delightful spot," he said, glancing out to sea and then at the end of his cigarette, which was only partially aglow. He puffed at it.

I said, "Yes," waiting for him to go on; presently he did.

"I am from the constabulary of this parish. The police, you see." And seeing my face, "This is a friendly call. But still it must be taken as a warning, Mister Norton. It is very serious. If anyone else comes to you about this it will mean trouble for you, heavy trouble. That's why I want to see you privately this way and warn you personally. You see."

I could not believe I was hearing his words. At length I said faintly: "But what about?"

"This is not an official call. You must not be upset. I have taken it upon myself to speak to you because I want to save you deep trouble."

"But I *am* upset!" I cried, finding my voice at last. "How can I help being upset, when I don't know what you're talking about?"

He moved his chair close to mine, and spoke in a very low voice.

"I have waited until the young man was away from the house so we could talk in private. You see, it is about him."

Somehow that did not surprise me. I nodded.

"I will tell you very briefly. The people here are simply country folk. They make trouble easily. Right now they are all talking about the young man you have living here with you. He is your son, I hear." His inflection here was sceptical.

"Certainly he's my son."

His expression did not change, but his voice grew indignant. "Whoever he is, that is a bad young man."

"What do you mean?" I cried, but he cut in hotly: "He may be your son; he may not be. I don't care who he is. That is not my affair. But he is bad through and through. We don't have such things going on here, sir. The people in Orange Walk and Saint Ives Cove are very cross now. You don't know what these folks do when they are aroused."

—
175

I thought it my turn to interrupt. "Please tell me why you say my son is bad. What has he done?" Perhaps the earnestness in my voice reached him, for his face assumed a gentler aspect. He leaned still closer to me and almost whispered.

"He has no shame. He does what he pleases with all the young boys, and the men too, and gives them a shilling so they won't tell about it. But they talk. Of course they talk. Every man for twenty miles up and down the coast knows about it. And the women too, they know about it." There was a silence.

I had felt myself preparing to get to my feet for the last few seconds because I wanted to go into my room and be alone, to get away from that scandalized stage whisper. I think I mumbled "Good morning" or "Thank you" as I turned away and began walking toward the house. But he was still beside me, still whispering like an eager conspirator into my ear: "Keep him home, Mister Norton. Or send him away to school, if he is your son. But make him stay out of these towns. For his own sake."

I shook hands with him and went to lie on my bed. From there I heard his car door slam, heard him drive off. I was painfully trying to formulate an opening sentence to use in speaking to Racky about this, feeling that the opening sentence would define my stand. The attempt was merely a sort of therapeutic action, to avoid thinking about the thing itself. Every attitude seemed impossible. There was no way to broach the subject. I suddenly realized that I should never be able to speak to him directly about it. With the advent of this news he had become another person—an adult, mysterious and formidable. To be sure, it did occur to me that the mulatto's story might not be true, but automatically I rejected the doubt. It was as if I wanted to believe it, almost as if I had already known it, and he had merely confirmed it.

Racky returned at midday, panting and grinning. The inevitable comb appeared and was used on the sweaty, unruly locks. Sitting down to lunch, he exclaimed: "Gosh! Did I find a swell beach this morning! But what a job to get to it!" I tried to look unconcerned as I met his gaze;

it was as if our positions had been reversed, and I were hoping to stem his rebuke. He prattled on about thorns and vines and his machete. Throughout the meal I kept telling myself: "Now this is the moment. You must say something." But all I said was: "More salad? Or do you want dessert now?" So the lunch passed and nothing happened. After I had finished my coffee I went into the bedroom and looked at myself in the large mirror. I saw my eyes trying to give their reflected brothers a little courage. As I stood there I heard a commotion in the other wing of the house: voices, bumpings, the sound of a scuffle. Above the noise came Gloria's sharp voice, imperious and excited: "No, mahn! Don't strike him!" And louder: "Peter, mahn, no!"

I went quickly toward the kitchen, where the trouble seemed to be, but on the way I was run into by Racky, who staggered into the hallway with his hands in front of his face.

"What is it, Racky?" I cried.

He pushed past me into the living room without moving his hands away from his face; I turned and followed him. From there he went into his own room, leaving the door open behind him. I heard him in his bathroom running the water. I was undecided what to do. Suddenly Peter appeared in the hall doorway, his hat in his hand. When he raised his head, I was surprised to see that his cheek was bleeding. In his eyes was a strange, confused expression of transient fear and deep hostility. He looked down again.

"May I please talk with you, sir?"

"What was all the racket? What's been happening?"

"May I talk with you outside, sir?" He said it doggedly, still not looking up.

In view of the circumstances, I humored him. We walked slowly up the cinder road to the main highway, across the bridge, and through the forest while he told me his story. I said nothing.

At the end he said: "I never wanted to, sir, even the first time, but after the first time I was afraid, and Mister Racky was after me every day."

—

I stood still, and finally said: "If you had only told me this the first time it happened, it would have been much better for everyone."

He turned his hat in his hands, studying it intently. "Yes, sir. But I didn't know what everyone was saying about him in Orange Walk until today. You know I always go to the beach at Saint Ives Cove with Mister Racky on my free days. If I had known what they were all saying, I wouldn't have been afraid, sir. And I wanted to keep on working here. I needed the money." Then he repeated what he had already said three times. "Mister Racky said you'd see about it that I was put in the jail. I'm a year older than Mister Racky, sir."

"I know, I know," I said impatiently; and deciding that severity was what Peter expected of me at this point I added: "You had better get your things together and go home. You can't work here any longer, you know."

The hostility in his face assumed terrifying proportions as he said: "If you had killed me I would not work any more at Cold Point, sir."

I turned and walked briskly back to the house, leaving him standing there in the road. It seems he returned at dusk, a little while ago, and got his belongings.

In his room Racky was reading. He had stuck some adhesive tape on his chin and over his cheekbone.

"I've dismissed Peter," I announced. "He hit you, didn't he?"

He glanced up. His left eye was swollen, but not yet black.

"He sure did. But I landed him one, too. And I guess I deserved it anyway."

I rested against the table. "Why?" I asked nonchalantly.

"Oh, I had something on him from a long time back that he was afraid I'd tell you."

"And just now you threatened to tell me?"

"Oh, no! He said he was going to quit the job here, and I kidded him about being yellow."

"Why did he want to quit? I thought he liked the job."

"Well, he did, I guess, but he didn't like me." Racky's candid gaze betrayed a shade of pique. I still leaned against the table.

I persisted. "But I thought you two got on fine together. You seemed to."

"Nah. He was just scared of losing his job. I had something on him. He was a good guy, though; I liked him all right." He paused. "Has he gone yet?" A strange quaver crept into his voice as he said the last words, and I understood for the first time Racky's heretofore impeccable histrionics were not quite equal to the occasion. He was very much upset at losing Peter.

"Yes, he's gone," I said shortly. "He's not coming back, either." And as Racky, hearing the unaccustomed inflection in my voice, looked up at me suddenly with faint astonishment in his young eyes, I realized that this was the moment to press on, to say: "What did you have on him?" But as if he had arrived at the same spot in my mind a fraction of a second earlier, he proceeded to snatch away my advantage by jumping up, bursting into loud song, and pulling off all his clothes simultaneously. As he stood before me naked, singing at the top of his lungs, and stepped into his swimming trunks, I was conscious that again I should be incapable of saying to him what I must say.

He was in and out of the house all afternoon: some of the time he read in his room, and most of the time he was down on the diving board. It is strange behavior for him; if I could only know what is in his mind. As evening approached, my problem took on a purely obsessive character. I walked to and fro in my room, always pausing at one end to look out the window over the sea, and at the other end to glance at my face in the mirror. As if that could help me! Then I took a drink. And another. I thought I might be able to do it at dinner, when I felt fortified by the whisky. But no. Soon he will have gone to bed. It is not that I expect to confront him with any accusations. That I know I never can do. But I must find a way to keep him from his wanderings, and I must offer a reason to give him, so that he will never suspect that I know.

—

We fear for the future of our offspring. It is ludicrous, but only a little more palpably so than anything else in life. A length of time has passed; days which I am content to have known, even if now they are over. I think that this period was what I had always been waiting for life to offer, the recompense I had unconsciously but firmly expected, in return for having been held so closely in the grip of existence all these years.

That evening seems long ago only because I have recalled its details so many times that they have taken on the color of legend. Actually my problems already had been solved for me then, but I did not know it. Because I could not perceive the pattern, I foolishly imagined that I must cudgel my brains to find the right words with which to approach Racky. But it was he who came to me. That same evening, as I was about to go out for a solitary stroll which I thought might help me hit upon a formula, he appeared at my door.

"Going for a walk?" he asked, seeing the stick in my hand.

The prospect of making an exit immediately after speaking with him made things seem simpler. "Yes," I said, "But I'd like to have a word with you first."

"Sure. What?" I did not look at him because I did not want to see the watchful light I was sure was playing in his eyes at the moment. As I spoke I tapped with my stick along the designs made by the tiles in the floor. "Racky, would you like to go back to school?"

"Are you kidding? You know I hate school."

I glanced up at him. "No, I'm not kidding. Don't look so horrified. You'd probably enjoy being with a bunch of fellows your own age." (That was not one of the arguments I had meant to use.)

"I might like to be with guys with my own, but I don't want to have to be in school to do it. I've had school enough."

I went to the door and said lamely: "I thought I'd get your reactions." He laughed. "No, thanks."

"That doesn't mean you're not going," I said over my shoulder as I went out.

On my walk I pounded the highway's asphalt with my stick, stood on the bridge having dramatic visions which involved such eventualities as our having to move back to the States, Racky's having a bad spill on his bicycle and being paralyzed for some months, and even the possibility of my letting events take their course, which would doubtless mean my having to visit him now and then in the governmental prison with gifts of food, if it meant nothing more tragic and violent. "But none of these things will happen," I said to myself, and I knew I was wasting precious time; he must not return to Orange Walk tomorrow.

I went back toward the point at a snail's pace. There was no moon and very little breeze. As I approached the house, trying to tread lightly on the cinders so as not to awaken the watchful Ernest and have to explain to him that it was only I, I saw that there were no lights in Racky's room. The house was dark save for the dim lamp on my night table. Instead of going in, I skirted the entire building, colliding with bushes and getting my face sticky with spider webs, and went to sit a while on the terrace where there seemed to be a breath of air. The sound of the sea was far out on the reef, where the breakers sighed. Here below, there were only slight watery chugs and gurgles now and then. It was unusually low tide. I smoked three cigarettes mechanically, having ceased even to think, and then, my mouth tasting bitter from the smoke, I went inside.

My room was airless. I flung my clothes onto a chair and looked at the night table to see if the carafe of water was there. Then my mouth opened. The top sheet of my bed had been stripped back to the foot. There on the far side of the bed, dark against the whiteness of the lower sheet, lay Racky asleep on his side, and naked.

I stood looking at him for a long time, probably holding my breath, for I remember feeling a little dizzy at one point. I was whispering to myself, as my eyes followed the curve of his arm, shoulder, back, thigh, leg: "A child. A child." Destiny, when one perceives it clearly from very near, has no qualities at all. The recognition of it and the consciousness of the vision's clarity leave no room on the mind's

—

181

horizon. Finally I turned off the light and softly lay down. The night was absolutely black.

He lay perfectly quiet until dawn. I shall never know whether or not he was really asleep all that time. Of course he couldn't have been, and yet he lay so still. Warm and firm, yet still as death. The darkness and silence were heavy around us. As the birds began to sing, I sank into a soft, enveloping slumber; when I awoke in the sunlight later, he was gone.

I found him down by the water, cavorting alone on the springboard; for the first time he had discarded his trunks without my suggesting it. All day we stayed together around the terrace and on the rocks, talking, swimming, reading, and just lying flat in the hot sun. Nor did he return to his room when night came. Instead after the servants were asleep, we brought three bottles of champagne in and set the pail on the night table.

Thus it came about that I was able to touch on the delicate subject that still preoccupied me, and profiting by the new understanding between us, I made my request in the easiest, most natural fashion.

"Racky, would you do me a tremendous favor if I asked you?"

He lay on his back, his hands beneath his head. It seemed to me his regard was circumspect, wanting in candor.

"I guess so," he said. "What is it?"

"Will you stay around the house for a few days—a week, say? Just to please me? We can take some rides together, as far as you like. Would you do that for me?"

"Sure thing," he said, smiling.

I was temporizing, but I was desperate.

Perhaps a week later—(it is only when one is not fully happy that one is meticulous about time, so that it may have been more or less)—we were having breakfast. Isiah stood by, in the shade, waiting to pour us more coffee.

"I noticed you had a letter from Uncle Charley the other day," said Racky. "Don't you think we ought to invite him down?"

My heart began to beat with great force.

—

"Here? He'd hate it here," I said casually. "Besides, there's no room. Where would he sleep?" Even as I heard myself saying the words, I knew that they were the wrong ones, that I was not really participating in the conversation. Again I felt the fascination of complete helplessness that comes when one is suddenly a conscious on-looker at the shaping of one's fate.

"In my room," said Racky. "It's empty."

I could see more of the pattern at that moment than I had ever suspected existed. "Nonsense," I said. "This is not the sort of place for Uncle Charley."

Racky appeared to be hitting on an excellent idea. "Maybe if I wrote and invited him," he suggested, motioned to Isiah for more coffee.

"Nonsense," I said again, watching still more of the pattern reveal itself, like a photographic print becoming constantly clearer in a tray of developing solution.

Isiah filled Racky's cup and returned to the shade. Racky drank slowly, pretending to be savoring the coffee.

"Well, it won't do any harm to try. He'd appreciate the invitation," he said speculatively.

For some reason, at this juncture I knew what to say, and as I said it, I knew what I was going to do.

"I thought we might fly over to Havana for a few days next week."

He looked guardedly interested, and then he broke into a wide grin. "Swell!" he cried. "Why wait till next week?"

The next morning the servants called "Good-bye" to us as we drove up the cinder road in the McCoigh car. We took off from the airport at six that evening. Racky was in high spirits; he kept the stewardess engaged in conversation all the way to Camagüey.

He was delighted also with Havana. Sitting in the bar at the Nacional, we continued to discuss the possibility of having C. pay us a visit at the island. It was not without difficulty that I eventually managed to persuade Racky that writing him would be inadvisable.

We decided to look for an apartment right there in Vedado for Racky. He did not seem to want to come back here to Cold Point. We also decided that living in Havana he would need a larger income than I. I am already having the greater part of Hope's estate transferred to his name in the form of a trust fund which I shall administer until he is of age. It was his mother's money, after all.

We bought a new convertible, and he drove me out to Rancho Boyeros in it when I took my plane. A Cuban named Claudio with very white teeth, whom Racky had met in the pool that morning, sat between us.

We were waiting in front of the landing field. An official finally unhooked the chain to let the passengers through. "If you get fed up, come to Havana," said Racky, pinching my arm.

The two of them stood together behind the rope, waving to me, their shirts flapping in the wind as the plane started to move.

The wind blows by my head; between each wave there are thousands of tiny licking and chopping sounds as the water hurries out of the crevices and holes; and a part-floating, part-submerged feeling of being in the water haunts my mind even as the hot sun burns my face. I sit here and I read, and I wait for the pleasant feeling of repletion that follows a good meal, to turn slowly, as the hours pass along, into the even more delightly, slightly stirring sensation deep within, which accompanies the awakening of the appetite.

I am perfectly happy here in reality, because I still believe that nothing very drastic is likely to befall this part of the island in the near future.

MS Ferncape
(New York–Casablanca)
1947

Harold Norse

Green Ballet

For W. I. Scobie

    overhead
    on the bridge
trucks are speeding under angels

parks are empty & leaves are falling

    erect in mud
    their shoes slurping
on the riverbank two people
are breaking laws with their hips

at the top of the steps a sign reads

    WORKERS ONLY   NO TRESPASSING

one is in rags
he is 16
he has red lips

the other is a man
who sees god as he looks up
    at the boy who looks down

the boy is thinking of the whore with the man
he spied on in the shadows

—

by Hadrian's Tomb
as he clutches the man's ears
          tensing his thick
thighs
      & they come

the man thinks *god god*
      & the terror!
any moment all's reversed
only the world's uniform THUD

all this time the Tiber sucking
    sucking
the fat mud

Rome, 1960

In Italian the title, *balletti verdi,* means gay scenes or scandals, in the vernacular.

John Giorno

Hi Risque

I want
to scat
in your mouth,
I want you
to scat
in my mouth,
I want to scat
on your face
and rub it in

chocolate,
caviar,
and champagne,
absolute
preliminaries
pushing
the inner
envelope
to the limit,
one more
time,
mining
diamonds
with your tongue
for the crown
of one
of the kings

of hell,
when the going
gets rough
the tough
get gorgeous

squeezing
money
from the air
squeezing money
from the air,
snake
tongue,
stretching
your tongue
to the Buddhas
diving
into the wreck
diving into
the wreck,
curiosity
and compassion,
and an exercise
in non-aversion,
fear
spiraling
from you
fear spiraling from you,
that gun's got
blood
in its hole

We do not do
this anymore,
but I still
think about it
when I'm
jerking off,
I was king
of promiscuity,
LSD,
crystal meth,
fist fucking
with 40 guys
for 14 hours,
it's worse
than I thought
and now,
every one
of them
I ever made
love to,
every single
one,
is dead,
and may they be
resting
in *great*
equanimity

We gave
a party
for the gods

and the gods
all came.

Allen Ginsberg

On Neal's Ashes

Delicate eyes that blinked blue Rockies all ash
nipples, Ribs I touched w/ my thumb are ash
mouth my tongue touched once or twice all ash
bony cheeks soft on my belly are cinder, ash
earlobes & eyelids, youthful cock tip, curly pubis
breast warmth, man palm, high school thigh,
baseball bicept arm, asshole anneal'd to silken skin
                all ashes, all ashes again.

August 1968

William Burroughs

"Sex as a biological weapon"

INTERVIEWER: Sex seems equated with death frequently in your work.

BURROUGHS: That is an extension of the idea of sex as a biological weapon. I feel that sex, like practically every other human manifestation, has been degraded for control purposes, or really for anti-human purposes. This whole puritanism. How are we ever going to find out anything about sex scientifically, when *a priori* the subject cannot even be investigated? It can't even be thought about or written about. That was one of the interesting things about [Wilhelm] Reich.* He was one of the few people who ever tried to investigate sex—sexual phenomena, from a scientific point of view. There's this prurience and this fear of sex. We know nothing about sex. What is it? Why is it pleasurable? What is pleasure? Relief from tension? Well, possibly.

* The psychologist Wilhelm Reich's books were burned by federal order in the 1950s (di Prima, etc.).

—

Allen Ginsberg

Rain-Wet Asphalt Heat,
Garbage Curbed Cans Overflowing

I hauled down lifeless mattresses to sidewalk refuse-piles,
old rugs stept on from Paterson to Lower East Side filled with bed-bugs,
grey pillows, couch seats treasured from the street laid back on the street
—out, to hear Murder-tale, 3rd Street cyclists attacked tonite—
Bopping along in rain, Choas fallen over City roofs,
shrouds of chemical vapour drifting over building-tops—
Get the *Times*, Nixon says peace reflected from the Moon,
but I found no boy body to sleep with all night on pavements 3 AM home
    in sweating drizzle—
Those mattresses soggy lying by full five garbagepails—
Barbara, Maretta, Peter Steven Rosebud slept on these Pillows years ago,
forgotten names, also made love to me, I had these mattresses four years
    on my floor—
Gerard, Jimmy many months, even blond Gordon later,
Paul with the beautiful big cock, that teenage boy that lived in
    Pennsylvania,
forgotten numbers, young dream loves and lovers, earthly bellies—
many strong youths with eyes closed, come sighing and helping me
    come—
Desires already forgotten, tender persons used and kissed goodbye
and all the times I came to myself alone in the dark dreaming of Neal or
    Billy Budd
—nameless angels of half-life—heart beating & eyes weeping for lovely
    phantoms—
Back from the Gem Spa, into the hallway, a glance behind

and sudden farewell to the bedbug-ridden mattresses piled soggy in dark rain.

August 2, 1969

Harold Norse

Now France

now france   yesterday italy   & it's fall
special paris light   slant on treetops   gray
buildingtops   clear   hard   like french eyes   bulge
of intellect   chalcedony eyes   slightly
      inhuman no?   & how
architecture creates   the sky

      will someone stop me in the street   saying
      how wonderful!   we don't know each other?!
        just walk arm in arm
        & never ask our names!
make love at sight!   anonymous as monks!
        esperanto lips!
      africa in my arms!   near east!

but how to slow down   i'm running away
      are those my arteries   or steel tracks?
        stations in the dawn   old man
sourly pushing letters   in huge sacks
      are they my unfinished plans?

      paris of leaves   beards   duffel coats!
    am i interested in radio telescopes?
    the kind that look inside the moon?
    parabolic mirrors?   limits of the solar system?
izvestia follows me around   sneers at my life
      no wonder i'm feeling blue

—

i'm here to tell you of a finer fate
    to explore trees
        listen to colors
            pick the golden flower
            feel under someone's duffel coat
                for the clear light
                of the void

down on your knees!   pray to the holy human body!
    worship god in the fork of the thighs!
        i can't blow the 'socialist vicory'
    nor raise any flag but my lilywhite ass
to all the silly nations who want me to choose sides

I've chosen   orgasm/feeling/smell/soul
freedom of dream   who is freer than when he dreams?
    i choose the light of the sky   over the boulevards
        & the bookstalls   full of sexy pictures
        & occult prophecies   THE EARTH

Allen Ginsberg

"Drag up your soul to its proper bliss..."

from an interview in the PARIS REVIEW, *1965*

...the only way you can be saved is to sing. In other words, the only way
to drag up, from the depths of this depression, to drag up your soul to its
proper bliss, and understanding, is to give yourself, completely, to your
heart's desire. The image will be determined by the heart's compass, by
the compass of what the heart moves toward and desires. And then you
get on your knees or on your lap or on your head and you sing and chant
prayers and mantras, till you reach a state of ecstasy and understanding,
and the bliss overflows out of your body.

William Burroughs

"The gay state"

from Howard Brookner's 1984 film WILLIAM BURROUGHS

The gay state, that's what I'm aiming for and I want us to be as tough as the Israelis. Anybody fucks around with a gay any place in the world we're gonna be there. [Cut.] Well we're a minority, why the hell don't we have the right to protect ourselves? [Cut.] We have to build up an international organization with false passports, guns on arrival, the whole lot, the whole terrorist lot. We are a precarious minority, we gotta fight for our lives. Do you understand? If they oppose the gay state we're going to find them, track them down and kill them. [Pauses to finish drink.] Why not?

* Excerpt from Jamie Russell's *Queer Burroughs*, 112.

Permissions

Grateful acknowledgment is made to the following for granting permission to reprint copyrighted material:

I. The Road of Excess (Or, Saintly Sinners)

Allen Ginsberg: "In Society," from *Collected Poems 1947–1980* by Allen Ginsberg. Copyright © 1984 by Allen Ginsberg. Reprinted by permission of HarperCollins Publishers Inc.

Herbert Huncke: "On Meeting Kinsey," from *The Herbert Huncke Reader.* Reprinted by permission of the Herbert Huncke Estate.

William Burroughs: "Nobler, I thought, to die a man than live on, a sex monster…" from *Queer* by William S. Burroughs, copyright © 1985 by William S. Burroughs. Used by permission of Viking Penguin, a division of Penguin Group (USA) Inc.

Alan Ansen: "Dead Drunk," from *Disorderly Houses,* copyright © 1961 by Alan Ansen, and reprinted by permission of Wesleyan University Press.

Herbert Huncke: "Youth," from *The Herbert Huncke Reader.* Reprinted by permission of the Herbert Huncke Estate.

William Burroughs: "I don't mind being called queer…" Letter to Allen Ginsberg; 4/22/52, from *Letters of William S. Burroughs: 1945–1959* by William S. Burroughs, edited by Oliver Harris, copyright © 1993 by William S. Burroughs. Used by permission of Viking Penguin, a division of Penguin Group (USA) Inc.

—

II. Male Muses (Or, Sex Without Borders)

III. Queer Shoulder to the Wheel

ABOUT THE AUTHOR

Regina Marler is the author of *Bloomsbury Pie: The Making of the Bloomsbury Boom* (Henry Holt, 1997) and the editor of *Selected Letters of Vanessa Bell* (Pantheon, 1993). She contributes to the *Los Angeles Times Book Review,* the *New York Observer,* and *The Advocate.* She lives a Beat life in San Francisco.